I0628480

H<u>ARDBOILED</u>
L.A. P<u>ULP</u>

SHORT STORIES OF HARDENED COPS IN A TOUGH TOWN

Copyright © 2011 Read Books Ltd.
This book is copyright and may not be
reproduced or copied in any way without
the express permission of the publisher in writing

British Library Cataloguing-in-Publication Data
A catalogue record for this book is available from
the British Library

Contents

Short Biographies of the Authors

THE EGYPTIAN LURE

Carroll John Daly

*　　*　　*

The zero night blasted a biting wind through the narrow streets of the lower city. But no dust or dirt, or the smells of the filthy streets came with it; they were embedded in the thick black ice that filled the gutters. Clear, crisp and biting—like the country air—the breath-taking wind cut into my face. An occasional scuttling, scurrying figure hustled from one doorway to another, or beat its way uncertainly along the pavement.

Once, beneath a dull light, a harness bull eyed me through watery lids. Half stepping out to block my passage, he thought better of it and waving his arms across his chest hurried along his beat. I knew the thought that ran through his mind—if he could drag in a drunk he could get warm while he was booking him. And I didn't blame him much. Still, that was the difference between him and me. I had business to attend to, or thought I had, and the old mercury could slip right out the bottom of the thermometer before I'd duck out on a job. The name of Race Williams stands for service.

Less than an hour ago, a boy had brought me an envelope full of money and there was a note requesting that I show up at a tough night-club as soon as possible. It spoke of trouble, and that I was taking my life in my hands, and had all the earmarks of an obituary column— without the place of my interment. It was just typewritten, and no name signed to it. But money talks, and here I was slipping along through the night to the 'Egyptian Lure'.

Now, I'm not exactly a child in arms, and I know there's a few hundred loose-thinking gunmen who'd be glad to try a pot shot at me. So the idea of a trap was not entirely from my mind. But I wouldn't disappoint the boys anyway. If they're willing to pay for a shot at me, why discourage the practice? Besides, there isn't any way to judge beforehand what's good business and what's bad. People that hunt me out aren't apt to be giving references. They're in trouble when they think of Race Williams. I'm a court of last appeal. Not exactly a private detective, though my licence so labels me. But the gilt letters on my office door spell—CONFIDENTIAL AGENT.

But—back to the street and the winter night and the temperature that was out to break all records. I found the 'Egyptian Lure'. It wasn't hard for me to locate the little door. I know the underworld well, and all its dives, and this place a blind man could find. Someplace below the street level, the tin pan notes of an over-ripe piano were clanging feebly against the insistence of a trap drum.

My eyes are accustomed to take in a picture quickly, and I got one that made my right hand slip to my overcoat pocket as I reached the dark, ill-smelling hallway which gave entrance to the so-called 'night-club'. For a figure had slipped back into the adjoining doorway, and two others had disappeared in the alleyway across the street.

Maybe there was nothing alarming in that, and maybe there was. It might be simply the big-hearted boyishness that makes one gangster wait to playfully knock over another, or it might be a reception committee for me. But if they intended to plug me from the darkness, they lost their chance almost the very second they had it. I'd swung through the outer door and was in the blackness of the hallway of the 'Egyptian Lure'. The next moment I was doing my stuff on the inner door—four, three and one—which was the regular knock of the preferred sucker list. If you didn't know the rap, a little shutter went open while you were looked over. They hated to lose a dollar in that joint. It was easy to get in if you had any money—harder to get out if you had any left. If you wanted a card of introduction, most any taxicab driver could furnish it.

The door opened slightly and I shot my foot within. I was fortunate as I stood in the dim light. The old bird on the door was a stranger to me.

'Just one—just one,' he muttered, as I slipped a bill into his hand. 'You're joining a party?' And he tried to stare into my face that was hidden by the slouch hat and turned-up collar.

'Just one.' I nodded at him. 'But I'll make a party of it before I leave.' And while he was thinking that one out I swung into the cloak-room, jerked the gun from my overcoat pocket to my hip, and parked my coat with the attendant. Then I turned, shot back my shoulders and stepped down the three steps into the dance hall.

The proprietor, a big oily Greek, labelled Nick, recognised me almost at once. His cheeks puffed, his eyes bulged and after rolling them around a bit he tried to smile as he finally led me to a little table in a dark corner of the room.

The whole room was a dismal affair, for that matter. Shaded, dirty lights, which were meant to give the effects of the soft Egyptian night, might have registered with that gang. But to me it looked more like the dingy, dirty cellar of old Madison Square Garden when the circus was in town. The paintings on the walls were a scream. Emaciated little camels rubbed noses with mangy lions and a dark-skinned warrior in gaily coloured robes overshadowed the pyramids, while a Pekingese dog in the background turned out on closer inspection to be the Sphinx. The atmosphere and the odours didn't have a whole lot on the Zoo, but it suited the crowd. Perhaps, after all, I don't know my geography and the smells of Egypt.

The proprietor bent over me.

'On pleasure, Mr Williams?' He tried to make his voice simply solicitous, but an anxious, alarmed note crept into his simple question. 'If you're not,' he added significantly, 'I'll have to speak to Joe.' And he jerked a thick thumb towards the huge bulk of the bouncer, who lounged behind the orchestra.

I laughed up at him—I couldn't help it. If I said I was there on business, he'd quit. This bird had seen me in action once before, when he was a waiter over on the Avenue. He knew if Joe tried to put me out of a dump like that, he'd put me out in a cloud of smoke. It may be pride on my part. But to be chucked out of there wouldn't help my business any nor my reputation. I'm not a mussy guy, you understand— but I don't lay down to have my face trampled all over either. Just one rule for the lad who starts a row with me. He must be prepared to finish it. I don't go in for horseplay.

But there stood the owner, Nick, ready to take my order—and when I gave it to him his face fell until his chin hung down on his chest.

'Bring me a split of White Rock,' I told him. 'And be sure the cap's tightly on. I carry my own opener.'

The hurt expression of his fat face, when he thought I'd questioned the honest intention of the house, lifted when I slipped him a five-case note—which was good pay for the water, but not too much if the cap was securely fastened. No—I didn't suspect the joint, but I hate to put anyone in the way of temptation.

'Now—beat it. You're blocking the show, and I'm all for a light fantastic evening.' I waved him aside.

And the show was on—such as it was. Five or six girls were shaking themselves loose from their clothes upon a small platform. There was the leading lady, who had seen her best days before McKinley was shot. But she had an arm on her like the sturdy oak and, so, could swing a mean chair if trouble started. Also her capacity for bum liquor could probably be rated in tank car lots. And that was a big asset. I daresay, through eyes of gin, her calcimined face looked like the Madonna's.

The younger ones were hand-picked and awkward. But the faces and figures stood out even through White Rock. Hard, speculative little faces, maybe, but pretty—that is, with a sinister sort of beauty. And I saw the one on the end.

She was two steps behind the others and about a note and a half off key in her song. Her eyelashes were blacker, her cheeks redder, and her golden curls the cheapest kind of a wig. Yet, she stood out. There was a fearful tightening of her lips and a ghastly grimace to the way they slipped back into what was meant for a smile. But the impression she left was that she didn't belong, and her flashing eyes searched the room with both fear and hope. A deadly terror one moment, the next a ray of hope. Her eyes told the story—nothing remarkable in that. I'm not especially gifted in reading faces, but hers was like an open book.

But I wasn't there to give the dames the up and up. I looked over the customers, and it was a queer crowd. Down near the stage were a half dozen college boys. At the next table a little pickpocket from the Avenue kept smiling at Nick, the proprietor, in an attempt to leave the impression that he was there simply on pleasure. Then, a flashy party from uptown, with high society stamped all over their dress shirts, and middle class stamped on their loud coarse mouths. There were a couple of stick-up men, spending the proceeds of their last haul—tipping lavishly and letting the crowd know that they were liberal guys. Yet, it wasn't hard to pick them out. Some I recognised, some were just stamped with the type—you can't miss them.

And I saw the two men who came in shortly after me—swarthy, dark fellows they were. Neither conspicuously dressed nor shabbily dressed. They were quiet, watchful men who, too, drank White Rock and eyed the performers with an absorbing interest and a certain sense of satisfaction that could hardly be built up on charged water. They neither applauded nor waved to the girls, but whispered occasionally to each other and nodded in apparent agreement. Instinctively, I knew that with these men my mission was connected.

The dance was over and the girls hopped from the platform and scurried about the room—greeting friends, acquaintances and strangers alike. It was a free and easy party. It was the girl on the end, with the tricky blonde wig, who came from the stage last. Uncertainly, she glanced about the smoke-laden room, then started down a narrow aisle between the rows of tables. I didn't watch her especially—I watched the dark men who now sat with their heads close together; their eyes upon the table, as if they made it a point to impress upon the performers that they did not desire their company.

It happened quickly, and I doubt if a single one in the room saw the motion. Even I, watching closely, could not be sure. But it seemed as if the blonde-wigged frail slunk close to the opposite tables as she passed the two men. It seemed, too, as if a thick brown hand shot out, closed upon the girl's wrist and pulled her to the table. Anyway, one thing was certain. She was sitting between the men and their grave demeanour had departed and they were laughing and talking and calling loudly for something to drink. In a dazed, uncertain, fascinated way the girl sat between them.

And I had something else to occupy my mind. A sharp-featured little performer had suddenly flopped into the seat beside me.

'How about a little drink, dearie?' A hand was laid upon my wrist. I shook her off.

'Beat it, kid,' I told her. 'I'm waiting for another Moll. She's jealous and has long nails.' That would save a long argument, and abuse for being a cheapskate. I know these dives and I know these women.

She laughed hoarsely, drew back slightly—and I heard her whisper, 'Race Williams.'

It was my turn to reach for her wrist now. Things were going to open up and the bank notes in the envelope be explained. I don't forget faces and this dame's map was strange to me. She wasn't sure, so she whispered my name.

'You want me?' I half pulled her closer. 'I'm Race Williams—you sent for me?'

'Not me! That girl over there,' she nodded vigorously towards the

6

girl who sat between the two men. 'The one with the Wops.' And if her words were not elegant they were at least expressive. Certainly those boys looked her description.

'She didn't know you—didn't dare ask who you were. I picked her up on the street three nights ago. She's scared of something, and I told her of you. She's dough heavy and I think those lads are looking for a split. Anyway she wants to chin with you, and she was afraid those Wops would try to stop her. My Gawd! they're giving her the walk now.'

And they were. They had jerked suddenly to their feet, with the girl between them. They didn't exactly drag her, and she didn't exactly go willingly; her feet sort of lifted and scraped alternately. But it didn't attract attention, for the two men leaned over her from either side, and they were laughing and talking as they hid her face behind their bobbing black heads.

She didn't scream and she didn't hold back, or if she did it wasn't noticeable. But there was my bank roll, being dragged off by two strangers.

'What's her name?' I asked the girl by my side quickly.

'Bernie—' She stopped a moment. 'Just Bernie, I guess. She's a good kid, and—'

But I didn't hear any more. Bernie had sent for me; Bernie had paid for action—and Bernie was going to get it. I snapped to my feet and turned towards the steps which led to the cloakroom.

I was just in time, for the men ahead with the girl between them ignored the cloakroom and were willing to brave the zero night without coats. Hardly thoughtful, for the girl's flimsy lace dress was built for the banks of the Nile. Of course, the cloakroom attendant made no effort to stop them. He had passed the stage where anything was strange to him.

One quick glance I took back over my shoulder, then stepped out quickly, shot past them, and turning stood before the trio in the dull light of the hall, between the cloakroom and the inner door.

'Why, Bernie.' I cocked one eye and played a lad with half a jag on. 'I thought I spotted the back of your neck. Not going, without having a drink with your little friend.' And then seeing the bewildered look in her eyes as she stared vacantly at me, I added, 'Thought you said you'd see me here tonight—said it, or wrote it, or something.' And this time I thought I got my wink over. At all events, the fear went out of her eyes—they shone once in that quick sparkle of hope

I'd seen on the platform, and she tried to speak. But no words came—her mouth just opened and closed, and her lips clicked with a dry snap.

'You'll pardon—my friend.' The big swarthy fellow attempted to push me aside. But the odds were against him. The hall was narrow, and besides, I'm not so easily pushed. 'The young lady is our friend. She feels not so well, and we are taking her home.'

'What—Little Bernie not well?' I still blocked the passage. 'She must have some medicine—got some real fine old stuff,' I babbled on, reaching for my hip. It was a hard game for me to play. Neither of these fellows knew me, and it might be to my advantage later on if they still thought me simply a drunk. Again—if the game was big enough and desperate enough and they suspected that I was not really talking through a bottle, an attack might come suddenly. It was in my mind to stick a gun into each man's ribs and bid them bye-bye. If there had been the slightest suspicion in their faces I would have done that little thing. But it was early in the game and I didn't want to misplay my cards. The smaller of the two men spoke for the first time.

'Get from before me.' And though there was no suspicion in his face, there was a threat in his words and in the hand that crept beneath his jacket.

'Little Bernie—going out in the cold—without no flannels.' I stammered on but I watched that hand, and I saw the knife before ever he raised it. I don't know if he intended to slip it between my ribs or if he was just going to threaten me with it. And I didn't wait to find out what was in his mind. My hand shot up; metal cracked against a protruding chin, and as they say in the movies—'the Italian sun went down'. The hall was narrow; he was close to the wall; and he did his stuff like a gentleman, slipping easily and softly to the floor.

There wasn't any use to fool after that. Somehow Bernie got a kick out of real action—fear or hope, or just good judgement. Anyway, she came to life, snapped out of the mechanical doll act, and with a quick jerk busted loose from her gentleman friend. That bird hesitated between following her, looking after his friend, or settling with me. 'He who hesitates is lost' may have its exceptions but this lad wasn't one of them. His face went through all the tricks of a pantomimist, right up to the point where he decided to pull a gun. And then I gave him the well-known rush—just a double grip and a swing about, and he was picking them up and putting them down in the most approved style. There are times, I suppose, when I do go in for light comedy. Since the popularity of the night-clubs the 'bum's rush' has come into style again.

The door man didn't hesitate. He may have thought I was the bouncer; his action may have been an involuntary one, but when he saw us coming towards him like that, he knew of but one thing to do. And he did it. He threw open the door, nodded at my final shove, and muttered something to himself as he closed the door again and slipped the lock home. The thing couldn't have come off better if we had had a dress rehearsal.

I turned back to the hallway. There was Nick, the proprietor, and he was shaking Bernie by the shoulders and demanding an explanation of the recumbent attitude of the paying guest upon the floor.

'Leave the kid alone.' I jerked Nick's hand roughly from the girl's shoulder. 'She's my girl friend. I came here to see her tonight. We want to talk. That bozo,' I pointed at the lad I had given the snore, 'wanted to go bye-bye with her.'

Nick's face started to show slight signs of intelligence. Besides, a couple were coming up the steps from the dance-hall, and the bulldog face of Joe, the bouncer, had appeared in the background.

'What's it to be?' I whispered quickly to Nick. 'A quiet evening or a riot? Make up your mind.' And I tapped my pocket significantly.

And Nick acted. He was all business and no mistake. His face cracked into smiles as he jerked out a hand and pulled a curtain, which hid the form upon the floor from the approaching couple.

'It is so, Mr Williams,' he finally said. 'Bernie is a lovely girl,' and he pinched her cheek. 'Perhaps you would wish a little drink with her in a private room.' He rubbed his hands together, patted me on the back, stepped to the people who were getting on their coats, and, after signalling Joe the bouncer, broke into loud laughter at some crude joke. But he kept the guests busy for the time it took Joe to slip behind the curtain.

Distinctly I heard feet scraping across wood, and a door slam. A moment of silence, and the curtains parted and Joe was in the hall again. He eyed me in unconcealed admiration.

'You must have slapped him an awful wallop.' He shook his head several times. 'He's as stiff as a mackerel.'

I simply nodded and smiled as I slipped the brass knuckles back in my pocket. Why give away the secrets of my trade?

Bernie stood trembling against the wall; the proprietor, Nick, was standing beside a little door which he held open. I took the girl by the arm and half led, half carried, her towards the narrow flight of stairs behind the open door. The smirking Nick winked and grimaced as we passed and slowly mounted the stairs. There are certain things I don't like, and the temptation was strong to give Nick a side swipe along his thick lips. But business must come before pleasure, and I might be able to use Nick before the night was over. Anyway, the door closed, and his fat, sensuous face was shut out.

'Come, Bernie,' I said, 'brace up—you're safe now.'

'Oh—oh,' she sobbed, and—'oh' again. And although there was deep feeling and great emotion behind the sobs, it sort of left me flat.

If she couldn't talk or walk very well, she was able to direct me along the dim narrow hall above to a shabby little private room. It took her a few minutes to get herself together, but finally she swung around, came towards me and opened up. If she couldn't talk before, she sure got off a chestful now.

'You came.' She busted right into a jumble of words. 'I knew those two men—recognised them, but, like a little fool, I didn't think that they'd know me. They only saw me once, and with the paint and wig and—But you were just in time.' Little hands crept around my neck, a blonde wig twisted itself upon my shoulder, and Bernie was telling me what hot stuff I was.

'Lay off the sex stuff,' I told her, as I pulled her arms away, and she sort of shot back and jerked her wig from her head. And Bernie was pretty. A little soap and water applied to that face would make her a knock-out. And I guess she saw the look of approval in my face. For she started in to do the vamp act again. A pitiful sort of effort it was, with the ghastly smile I had seen on the platform. Bernie wasn't bad—she was good. There was the sparkle of youth to her eyes that fear hadn't killed yet—a sparkle that no number of beauty doctors can put in the eyes of a soul that is bad. Bernie just hadn't met the right kind of boy friends—that was all. So I'd put her right, on the time she was wasting.

'Yes, you're pretty, Bernie.' I looked straight at her. 'Maybe beautiful—and I daresay you have a bagful of cute tricks. But put them back in the bag. You have sent me money and I have come to help you. You might be cock-eyed and have a hare lip and an ear or two that had been gewed up by a gentleman friend. It wouldn't make any difference. You've paid cash for service—you're going to get it. What do you want?'

Her hands were half in midair and hung there until I finished, then they dropped to her side. The lips ceased to quiver; the black eyes widened slightly as she weighed my words.

'You will help me—regardless?' she finally asked.

'Regardless of what? Those boys downstairs?'

At the mention of them the fear shot back into her face again. 'Will you—can you get me out of this place?'

'Absolutely,' I told her, and meant it.

'These are desperate men—they would have taken me by force tonight—they would have killed you without hesitating. They would kill you without thought.'

'But they'll give considerable thought to it after they make the first attempt.' I smiled down at her. And then, 'Why didn't you call out when they led you from the room tonight? You were too frightened?'

'Yes,' she said quickly, and then—her cheeks whitening beneath the rouge—'Partly that; but I was afraid.'

'Of what?'

She hesitated; and I cut in again.

'Of the police, Bernie?' I asked.

And this time she jerked back against the table.

'How did—you know that?' she stammered.

Mind reading? Maybe. But I simply smiled. People who don't fear the police for some reason or other, don't want me. Bernie very easily could have hollered herself in a cop or two most any time, yet she hadn't. And the answer, of course, was that she didn't want one.

'It is true.' She finally cocked her head up half defiantly. 'But I am not bad—or if I was it was for a good purpose—an all-compelling purpose. You will not help me?'

'There are laws and laws,' I told her. 'I have my own ethics and I am my own judge of right and wrong. But I'll do this for you. I'll see you safely away from here. I won't help you beat the law, without knowing the facts—but I'll help you beat this gang you fear.'

'How much must I tell you?'

'As little or as much as you please.'

'How much must I pay you?' She hesitated.

'You have paid enough for that service. If you want to open up later, why—'

'I want to tell you now,' she cried suddenly. 'I don't want you thinking I'm bad. My mother was an Italian, but I am an American. I was born in this country. My father died—my mother sang upon the stage. There was money from my father, and I went to a convent in

Italy. Then from a doctor I received word that my mother was sick and might die. I had little money, but enough—so I went to Naples to sail for New York. And there I was robbed—there, with the boat about to sail, I was without money—and my mother dying.' She wiped away a tear—real stuff, too—and continued:

'There I met a lady to whom I confided my trouble. She helped me—arranged my passage—but I must do something for her. So I became bad. I smuggled in some diamonds. I knew it was wrong; I knew that I shouldn't—but I did it. My mother was dying. That is my crime. That is my secret, for which I pay money to hide. My guardian helped me. And then I began to fear him and think that perhaps he had so arranged things. And he used my money, and his eyes burned when they watched me, and once, when I would run away—but enough—'

'Who is your guardian, Bernie—and what is his name?' I asked her.

'I think—all that I shall not tell. I only wish to run away and hide myself. From time to time I can send him money, and he may be satisfied and leave me alone. But I have seen him talk friendly with one I considered my enemy—one who received money to keep my secret. The tall man below, whom I have heard called Ferganses—the one you put out the door. You see, I fear him; I fear my guardian; and I fear this government that would punish me for my crime, for they did not know and would not understand my desire to see my mother. But my mother had died before I reached New York.' And she started in to turn on the water works again.

'You have money, Bernie—much money?'

'It is considerable. I could stand it no longer. I ran away, but I did not know where to go. My guardian had sent me to the bank, and I drew out a large sum of money and left. Then I was afraid—and I met a girl who was kind and brought me here. They must have suspected—sought me out. This girl spoke of you, and I sent for you.'

I could have laughed, but I didn't. Bernie's face made it all ring with sincerity. Poor kid—no doubt this guardian was behind the whole show and played the fear of the government up in her imagination. It wouldn't be hard—Bernie had 'convent' written all over her. To her it was a horrible crime. It was certainly lucky that Bernie got me instead of some private detective who'd prey on her fears and take most of her money to straighten things out with the government. But I don't play the game that way. I'd soon put her wise that her fears were groundless. I know the ropes and I know men, and I know a good fixer.

'Bernie,' I started—and stopped, swung about suddenly and flung open the door. It was with considerable effort that Nick, the proprietor, saved himself from pitching forward upon the floor.

'Well—' I jerked him erect. 'Why the Little Bo Beep act?'

'You—joke,' he stammered—caught his breath and faced me with a scowl. 'I should go for the police,' he snapped suddenly. 'If I had known why you came here, Race Williams, and what trouble you would bring my house, I—But you must go at once—I will help you.'

'Why must we go?' I watched that shrewd, fat face with its mean, snapping little eyes.

'Because him you thrust out has returned. He demands that this girl come to him. He is of your disposition, and threats.'

'Why not send for the police?' There was one thing certain about Nick—he'd take care of himself.

'I do not desire the police here. This is an honest club; but people lie about it, and the reputation must not get too bad. Besides, then I would make an enemy of three divisions—the police, these people who seek the girl, and you.'

I understood that point of view all right. Certainly, Nick and the police would have little in common. As for me, perhaps he was right there, too. Bernie and I didn't seek the cops. But the others; if I went with the girl they wouldn't be any too friendly towards Nick. And he straightened that point out before I could put the question to him.

'Come—I wish for peace,' he shot in on my thoughts. 'You take her out the back way. I want not to see her face some more. Then, you are satisfied with Nick; then these strangers can be convinced that she did not linger here, but went at once. But hurry.'

'Can we get out the back without being seen?'

'It is so. When I am notified of raids, it is through the alley in the back that the guests leave. Shall I show you?'

And I guess he could. These people were strangers to Nick's place—they would not know of the back way. Or would they? But I shrugged my shoulders. Bernie and I would do our stuff out the rear entrance. The next move was up to them. If those fellows couldn't shoot any straighter than they talked, they'd regret their lack of education.

Nick led the way down the long hall to the rear of the building. He was in a hurry and nervous. Guess he must have remembered that bit of gun play on the Avenue, when he was a waiter. Another thing—Nick was the sort that could see a nickel a mile, and here he was helping me show a clean pair of heels to Bernie's little playmates without asking a cent for it. That wasn't like Nick, and I chuckled inwardly. It all went to show how anxious he was to see the last of me.

Yet, with all his anxiety, he was prepared to see that no time was lost. Over his arm was swung a heavy, hooded cape for the girl, and he had also brought my coat and hat.

We passed some place back of the music, took a quick twist, and stood in a dark, cold little vestibule. Outside, the wind whistled and the zero night crept between the cracks, and through the dirty, musty glass above the door were the outlines of buildings—the lower city's tenements. Here and there was a small patch of the blue sky reflected behind the sharp brightness of half a dozen stars. The night was as clear and bright as it could be without a moon.

I slipped into my coat and jerked on my hat. Nick threw the cape about the girl's shoulders and pulled the hood well down over her head so that it hid her face. It was too or three sizes too big for her, but Nick explained that—as if he had thought the whole thing out.

'Others leave hurriedly by this little door,' he said. 'Sometimes wives, with detectives, come seeking divorce evidence—and we have such a hurried exit of a couple. So, if they suspect this way, they cannot be sure. If you desire you can look and see if it is safe—then be gone.'

Not half bad advice that. I turned to Bernie.

'You stand here.' I pulled her close to the door as I carefully jerked it open and slipped out into the stone yard behind. Then I shut it, all but an inch. 'If you hear anyone coming or get afraid of anything let out a holler,' I cautioned her. 'Don't be afraid to scream. We're only going quietly for the sake of dear old Nick. I won't be far.' So I gave the kid's hand a squeeze of encouragement. It was cold, and trembled in my grasp.

And I didn't go far; the night was clear enough. There was just a few feet to the little alleyway between two fences, and this alley led down to the yard behind. I couldn't be sure, but I thought that I made out a door between the two fences, in the back. Not a soul in sight—no place in the alley for a man to hide. Several places in the square of yard, though, for it was a dirty litter of barrels and boxes. It would have taken a half-hour to look behind all of them, and while you were looking behind one a hidden enemy could pop up behind another. No—I wouldn't waste the time. It would take just a few seconds to rush Bernie the distance to the alley, which was protected on both sides by the high fence. Nick had, no doubt, built that extra height of board fence for the convenience of suddenly departing guests.

One more quick glance I took down the alley—and turned, listening. There was no sound but the dull hum of the music and the scraping of feet across the dance-hall floor. I looked towards the door—it was still slightly open—and the music stopped. Not a sound in that vestibule, so I finished my 'look-see' in the alley. The coast was clear. I didn't waste any time getting back to Bernie.

The girl was there, leaning close to the door and back against the wall—dimly I made out her figure, the size of it triply accentuated in the wrap and the hood which hid even the whiteness of her face. And Nick—nervously his feet were pawing the ground, and his breath was coming in great sucking sounds.

'Listen, Bernie—you must brace up now. You are safe.' I encouraged the girl, who leaned against the wall. I think that she nodded, but it was too black there to be sure. But she did not speak.

'Tell me if you can walk it—' I started, and stopped. Footsteps were in the hall behind us. There was an angry voice, a quick curse, and a sudden pound against the wall—as if two men struggled.

But I didn't hear any more. Nick had jerked open the back door, and once again Bernie broke into life. She grabbed suddenly at my wrist and dragged me after her into the night—and I didn't have to guide her. She must have had real fear of these people, and she knew how to go, too, for I had hardly time to jerk a gun into my hand before we were in the alley and beating it down the straight stretch between the two fences. It just goes to show that you don't know women. I'd have been willing to bet, a minute before, that she would blow up and I'd have to carry her.

She held my hand now, and hers wasn't cold any longer. It was warm and moist, and her legs didn't sag—they were real speedy. She seemed to know, too, where the gate was and how it opened, but perhaps she had come that way before—perhaps the girl who had spoken to me at the table wised her up to all the little ins and outs of Nick's establishment. But what did it matter? Here we were in a straight line for the street beyond. And even then she didn't pause. A taxi was passing. The driver saw us reach the sidewalk, flung open the door—and we were in. Certainly she had all the luck, if it was simply luck.

That taxi being there was more than luck—at that time of night. It was almost like an act of Providence—and I believe in Providence as much as the next fellow, maybe—but I don't believe in Providence furnishing taxicabs at two o'clock in the morning. Yet, if the taxicab was there to inveigle us into it, what good would that do the swarthy gentleman and Bernie's kindly disposed guardian? There was only one man on the driver's seat, and his back was towards me. Surely he wasn't childish enough to think that he could run off with me.

'Where to?' the driver said, slipping into second. And then added: 'You got a lucky break. I got your message right. You can count on me any time, Boss,' he finished, with a touch of pride.

Now that didn't sound like a trap. Of course the taxi had been arranged for. But by whom? Nick? Yes, I suppose so. Nick certainly did things quick and thoroughly.

'Nick got you all right.' I fell in with the driver's spirit as I told him to slip along uptown.

'I don't know if it was Nick.' The driver shook his head. 'I just come back from a trick and got the message out front.'

And that was that. I turned to the girl, who had started in the vamp stuff again. She clung to me like a drunk to a lamp-post when I tried to push her away, and when I asked her where she'd like to go she simply grunted. Yep—grunted, is right.

'You're safe now.' I gave her a pat on the back and told her to lay off the parking business, and as I turned my head I got a whiff of her breath—and it startled me. It reeked of whisky, and I hadn't noticed that before—but I wouldn't in the cold. And, boy, I got a real shock, for I suddenly remembered that Bernie had clung around my neck in the heat of the private dining-room and that she didn't gag me with her breath then. And surely she hadn't tanked up in the moment I—And I knew. I pushed the girl from me, roughly knocked down her arms and jerked her head up. We passed a street lamp, but I didn't need one. I knew even before I glanced into that map. The girl in the taxi with me was not Bernie. I had been taken in like a child.

I don't cry over spilt gin—and I don't holler when I'm hurt. I just had the driver pull the car to the kerb, and I flung open the door.

'Get out!' And when she didn't move fast enough I picked her up and sat her on the pavement. I knew now why this girl made such good tracks down the alley, and I knew why the hand was warm instead of cold. Should I have been suspicious? I should have. For I had had one real opportunity to suspect that things were fishy, and that was Nick's not asking for a hand-out. He always wanted money for every little thing—why not a big one like this?

It was all simple—so simple that I nearly boiled over. There had been another girl and another cape. A hand over Bernie's mouth—and another girl in her place. Just a matter of seconds, and while I was looking down that alley there were many. It only goes to show you how much we misjudge human nature. I didn't think for a moment that Nick had the guts to double-cross me like that. And I had been proud because he was so anxious to get rid of me. 'Pride goeth before a flop' must have been written for me.

But the girl on the sidewalk was putting up an awful squawk, and the taxi driver was turning in his seat and looking at me reproachfully.

'Drive on,' I told him, and there must have been something in my voice that made him realise I meant business. The girl, too, seemed to understand, for her tough little face slunk from view as I slammed the door. And if it hadn't—well, I like to pose as a gentleman, so we won't go into the probable damage to the taxi when that door swished through the air.

This time when the driver asked me 'Where to?' I had a definite point of destination.

'Back to the "Egyptian Lure",' I said simply.

Oh, I've often blown about my sense of humour, but I didn't laugh then. I just sat back in the cab and thought, and my thoughts were not pleasant. At least, they shouldn't have been pleasant—but I think I got some satisfaction over the little surprise I promised Nick.

And Nick would tell that story around, and Race Williams would be the laughing stock of the Avenue! Good enough. They could have their laugh—that is, all of them but Nick. But most of all, my pride was hurt—and I had paraded my courage and confidence and ability before Bernie. Where was my boasted service now? And Bernie's money was in my pocket.

Was she in actual danger? Was she back with her guardian or still at Nick's? But I didn't believe she was still at Nick's. Then why was I going to Nick's? I tapped the driver on the shoulder.

'Pull up for a minute,' I said, 'and don't disturb me. I'm going to think.' And if he got a laugh out of that last crack, he got it to himself.

Why was I going to Nick's? That was the question I had to answer. If it was simply for private vengeance, then I was wrong. My duty now more than ever was to Bernie. Nick had double-crossed me. But why? Money? Certainly. Was Nick in the game all the way through? No— the coincidence would be too great for that. He didn't know the reason, and he didn't know the men, maybe. He worked as he always worked— blindly, on the size of the bank roll. But perhaps he knew where Bernie was. Oh, they wouldn't tell him, and he'd deny it to me. But I knew

Nick—he'd look for more money in the game, and he'd probably try to follow the car that Bernie went away in. And if he succeeded he'd tell me—maybe he thought he wouldn't, but he would. There wouldn't be a cent in it for him either. I have most persuasive ways. I set my teeth grimly—ten minutes before, I'd strutted before Bernie like a game-cock; now—I tapped my gun. I'd find Nick and stick that forty-four down his throat, even if he had Joe the bouncer and all the other waiters in the establishment ready for me.

'Drive on,' I said to the chauffeur, and this time our destination hadn't changed much. I was still going to the 'Egyptian Lure'—but I'd stop the car around the block and get out. Nick had taken me in like a child—well, I'd play the child's game and make this visit a surprise party.

'Listen, Big Boy,' I told the driver as I slipped a few yellow-backs into his hand, 'this is for telling a bed-time story—any you wish. I want to know if Nick's at the club. If he isn't, I want you to tell me when he gets back. If he asks about me, strike him for a tip; tell him I got out of the cab and raised hell, and left you. I'll wait in the doorway around the corner.'

'You'll freeze to death, mister.' He shook his head.

'Not me—' I told him. But if I had added that I was so hot that the perspiration was pouring down me, he wouldn't have believed it. Anyway, I was hot under the collar.

I didn't threaten this lad with what I'd do to him if he put it over on me. He wasn't that sort of a bird. I simply promised to double the fistful of jack I'd given him if he made good. There was no use in my going to the 'Egyptian Lure' if Nick wasn't there. And if he was out snooping on Bernie's little playmates, it was ten to one he'd ring up to find out if I'd come back before he returned.

Perhaps Bernie needed me at once. Perhaps Bernie was in danger. Yet I could not afford to hurry things. I must give Nick a chance to get the information I needed. Of course, it might be possible to work back over the ground and track down the two swarthy boys who had grabbed Bernie in the restaurant, and so find her. But that would take time. No—for a bit I must move cautiously—cautiously, until I was sure—and then strike. I clenched my teeth tightly. What a fine mutton-head I had been!

The taxi had gone. The little narrow street was empty, and the hallway I shivered in, a dismal, cold, damp place. Twice I looked out, but there was no sign of a taxi, but the third time the street was not entirely deserted. Down the block a figure dashed from an alleyway, looked up and down the street—then, turning, ran quickly along the sidewalk in the opposite direction from my hiding-place.

For a moment I stood there watching the fleeing figure. But there was nothing odd in that. A criminal? Maybe. The lower city is full of them. A derelict—a poor, homeless creature of the night? Probably; just frightened out of a sleep in a rubbish heap. And I got a glimpse of those broad shoulders and a fleeting vision of his face as he passed beneath a street lamp.

It jarred me erect and out on to the sidewalk. Imagination? Maybe. The thing was on my mind, of course. But the man who sped down the street was strangely like the swarthy man whom I had helped out of Nick's some time before; the man Bernie had called Ferganses. As I say, maybe it was a mind picture; certainly there was little else under my hat. Anyway, I was out of that doorway and speeding after him.

Whether he was my man or not made little difference. He heard me, or saw me, almost at once—for his head darted quickly back over his shoulder. There was a brownish-white face in the darkness, and he increased his speed. Whatever his purpose, it wasn't an honest one.

The chase was hopeless from the beginning. He was around the corner before I was half-way down the block. I heard the throb of a racing motor—the grinding of gears, and when I reached the corner the street was deserted. Maybe a car had been waiting for him—maybe he had disappeared in any of the numerous tenements—and maybe, again, he was not my man at all. But if he was, what business did he have in the alley a few houses down from the hallway where I had parked?

So I retraced my steps. The run had done me good; warmed up my body and cooled off my head. I'd have a 'look-see' in that alley. And it was like most other alleys of the lower city. Garbage-cans piled along the sides and the little yard in the back—cans that might stay there until a sensitive nose from the health department drifted by.

There was a printing shop in front and the rear yard was full of boxes. I looked up at the tenement windows above—all dark. Yet I dared not use a light, and there was no moon. I stumbled over the thing before I saw it. A foot—a human foot, with the shoe protruding from beneath some boxes.

I'm not easily thrilled or shocked and I am entirely without nerves—but I'm willing to admit that I got at least a kick out of that foot. There wasn't enough light to tell me if it was the foot of a man or a woman—

just the dull outline of the shoe and the feel of the ankle as I kicked it. And my heart did a jump—neither of fear nor horror—sort of a conscience twinge of remorse. For I thought of Bernie and the fear she felt.

I knelt on the ground and removed the boxes from the body. It wasn't Bernie. The figure was too bulky and the clothes were a man's—black, but for the generous expanse of white stiff shirt. One hasty glance at the windows above and I jerked out my flash. Just a single instant the bright rays lit on that stiff white-bosomed shirt and the patch of red with the handle of a knife sticking from the centre of it. There was a pudgy hand, too, with fingers clenched across the body. Then the sharp brilliancy rested on the face—pasty, greasy white, with wide, staring, sightless eyes. Enough is enough, and sometimes too much. When I jerked myself to my feet I knew that I wouldn't get any information from the lips of Nick. I had planned vengeance on the poor, money-grabbing Greek—now, that was forgotten. Nick had double-crossed me. To the old proverb, 'The way of the transgressor is hard,' might be added another line—'also speedy'. They don't come much deader than Nick.

I experienced no sense of satisfaction that Nick had paid the price. It only made me feel just how badly I had erred—how real were the fears of Bernie—and just what danger the poor kid must be in. But why had they killed Nick? What had he learned? Did he know who this guardian was? Had he followed the man and found out? But all that would take time. Then what—had the guardian himself come to the 'Egyptian Lure'? Had he approached Nick earlier in the night? But all that was only guesswork. One thing was sure. Nick had tried to follow them, and Nick had been caught and killed and probably dragged into the rear yard.

Had he gained any information—had he—? And I flashed on the light again, for I remembered seeing Nick's hand and the tightly closed fist when my flash first went to work. It took real force to open those fingers, but I did it and got out a piece of paper. It was crumpled into a tiny ball. I slipped it into my pocket. Then I turned quickly and left the alley.

I didn't wait for my taxi driver to return. I didn't need the information that Nick wasn't at the 'Egyptian Lure' and I wasn't afraid that the taxi driver would mix me up with this bit of murder when it was discovered. Not him. His kind don't talk. His life was hardly an open book and wouldn't stand investigation. If the police did connect him with Nick and his business the night of the murder—well—I shrugged my shoulders. It wouldn't be the first time I had come under an official investigation, and I guess it wouldn't be the last.

I was five blocks away when I spread open that bit of paper. And there was something in it. The enemy was right in suspecting that Nick had followed them for a purpose; but they were wrong in suspecting that he used his head. Nick always had a bad head for figures. But there were numbers written on that sheet of paper. And I didn't need any Sherlock Holmes to tell me that the numbers were the licence of an automobile—the automobile that Bernie was carried off in. I felt a little better as I shoved the paper back in my pocket. Bernie was going to see me strut my stuff again—and this time we were going to get action.

I didn't have much fear that the licence number would be a fake one. They didn't know that I was in the case until Nick told them—if he did. The enemy had just tracked Bernie down and intended to drag her from her hiding-place. They didn't suspect she had consulted anyone, and there was no reason for them to believe that they would be watched or followed. That had all come later. They were gentlemen who met unexpected problems when they came to them—met them thoroughly and efficiently. As a witness to that efficiency was the cold, dead body of Nick stretched out in the alley yard.

The next day I had the desired information about that licence. There was a real kick in the foreign label of the lad who owned the car. Doctor Antonio Maderia. It made me rub my hands together. The name was certainly in tune with Bernie's story and the two gents who had tried to drag her from the night-club. Now, we'd have a slant at the bird with the fancy moniker and see if he'd like to teach me any playful tricks with a knife.

Doctor Antonio Maderia hung his hat in a brownstone front well uptown. There was a sign in the window that modestly designated his profession and pointed out that he saw patients by appointment only. Well—I didn't have any appointment, but then—I didn't intend to be a patient.

A female chirped as the door opened.

'You have an appointment with the doctor?' And I drew a bit of a shock at the trim little maid who answered the door. I didn't exactly expect to be greeted by a lad with a blackjack in one hand, a gun in the other, and a knife between his teeth. But I did expect to find a lad who could hold his own in a fight.

She frowned; told me that the doctor was busy over some work, but finally, when I was persistent, agreed to take in my card. I made no bones about that card—there was no necessity for Doctor Maderia to peek through a hole in the door to see who was asking for him. I'm not ashamed of my name, and RACE WILLIAMS stood out like a sore thumb in the centre of the white pasteboard. This doctor would grab himself off an eyeful and no mistake.

Only a minute or two I waited in the hall before he came down. He was a tall, rangy bird, with sharp features and uncertain eyes that were sunk far back in his head. They were dull sort of eyes but for the steel-like points in the centres of them, and he sort of bent his head forward and looked up at me, tapping the card nervously in his hand.

'Mr Williams,' he said at length, 'we will talk in here.' And I followed him into a little room off the hall. Before he shut the door he pulled up all the shades, flooding the room with light. Then he turned again and looked at me, and looked at the card.

'"Confidential Agent",' he said after a bit. 'You are a detective then. You are not going to tell me that something has happened to Bernie.'

Now, you'll admit that was a good start—the opening words of a man who has nothing to fear. But if it was a monkey wrench he was trying to toss into my works, it missed the machinery. I eyed him placidly.

'Yes—' I looked him straight in the eyes. 'You are her guardian, I believe.'

'In a way—in a way.' He tapped his fingers upon the chair. 'Nothing legal, you understand. She was alone and abroad. Her mother—well, I knew her. She was of my country and she asked me to look after the girl, before she died. She is of age, of course. I have tried to advise her at times.'

'She lived here with you?'

'Yes, that is so,' he said, after a moment's hesitation. 'She lived here with me.'

'And you helped straighten out her mother's estate?'

'There was little to straighten.' He smiled. 'Stocks and bonds and a savings bank account.'

'You charged her for such service, of course.'

'But, no.' He shook his head. 'There was really nothing to do. I have enough for my own needs—and her inheritance was trivial.'

'She told me it was considerable.' I fired the statement straight at him.

'So—' He stroked his chin with long, thin fingers. 'Perhaps it was to her. And now,' he broke in before I could fire another question, 'you have come here, taken up my time and questioned me. May I ask just why I am indebted to you for this visit?'

'I have come,' I said, 'to see Bernie—where is she?'

And he was on his feet at once.

'Ah—' His eyes flashed far back in his head. 'So you waste my time. I tolerated your presence, Mr Williams, because of the girl. I thought you brought information. Now—you would question me. I have helped her and advised her, and she has repaid me by leaving my house suddenly—three days ago. What, might I ask, do you know about her?'

And I quit beating about the bush.

'I know enough to know that she's in trouble. I know enough to know that she fears you. And I know that you threaten her with a secret. And I know that she left your house in fear, and that you followed her and found her and carried her away. And I know—' I stopped suddenly and raised my right hand that was sunk deep in my overcoat pocket. 'I also know,' I said very slowly, 'that if the lad who is so carefully opening that door behind you don't close it again, there'll be a mess on the carpet.'

And the door closed with a click—and Doctor Maderia's face whitened. I had struck my first blow.

'The maid—' he stammered, as he turned towards the door.

I stretched out a hand and stopped him.

'It's no use, Doctor.' I took advantage of my first blow and followed it up quickly. 'I don't know the whole game, but I know enough of it. The girl did wrong—probably inveigled into it. How you worked it is not my business. How to prove it on you is not my business. I'm here only in the interest of Bernie. Produce the girl—cut the blackmail, and the dead body of Nick is up to the police. Otherwise—' I finished with a shrug. 'They burn 'em in this state.'

The doctor's back was half to me, but I could see the side of his face, and he was weighing the possibilities. At length he turned—and the whiteness was gone from his cheeks. He was the calm, dignified physician who had entered the room a few minutes before.

'You confuse me, Mr Williams.' Again those long, delicate fingers swept over his face. 'And I do not know exactly how to answer you— your accusation can hardly be ignored. I am hesitant—undecided whether I should simply show you the door and let the police take care of the whole muddle.' He paused a moment—then, 'I am willing to discuss the matter further. You have seen the girl and she has spoken to you. May I understand just what she had told you? Certainly she has had trouble—and we must make allowances. You have discovered Bernie's secret and you wish to be paid for silence.'

And I just laughed that one off. But if he wanted the cards laid on the table I'd lay them for him. And I did. I told him I had seen the girl. I told him that I knew she had smuggled in rocks. I told him how Nick had died, and I told him of the piece of paper in Nick's hand. And he listened to the evidence like a learned judge.

'You have made quite a case against me, Mr Williams.' He smiled. 'But it seems to rest on facts that are weak. If the police had found that licence number I would have something to explain, perhaps. And if the girl was to tell her story again I would have something to explain. But since the police did not find the paper and the girl does not come forward to tell her story, things are rather awkward.

'Bernie committed a wrong. I have helped her hide it. Another held her secret. Blackmail has been paid—and then she ran away. That is my story to you and my story to the police. Not a pleasant one—I admit I have been foolish.'

'And you deny that the girl is here or that you know where she is?'

'Absolutely.'

'And if I wish to search the house?'

He frowned slightly, and then:

'I do not think that under the circumstances I would deny you that. And I think that I shall tell you a few facts. Perhaps, then, you will believe that I have been wronged. Bernie is weak of character. I believe that when her mother died she was without funds and in Italy. A young Italian whom she met offered her her passage in return for smuggling in diamonds. We will give her credit for wishing to see her mother before she died. Her secret was discovered. A man followed her to this country and blackmailed her. She confided in me. I advised seeking lawyers—but, no. She paid, and I assisted her. At least I could hold their demands in check by threatening to tell the police. Personally, I had little to fear. Somehow, Bernie got the illusion that I was helping them. But—there, you do not believe me. She ran away. I have not seen her since. And the car, which number you have, she took with her.'

Bull? Probably. But he had one advantage over me. My threats were useless. If I went to the police, what would become of the girl? Her smuggling didn't amount to near-beer. I could straighten that out. But this doctor knew where the girl was and was keeping her a prisoner. What then? The thing behind it all was big enough for him to go in for murder. Since you can't electrocute a man more than once, why should he hesitate about shoving Bernie over? She'd make a tough witness against him. Still, my game wasn't to roast this duck; my game was to save the girl.

It was in my mind to shove a rod into his mouth and threaten to blow him off if he didn't tell me where the girl was. But it couldn't work out that way. Somehow I had the impression that I was sitting on a keg of dynamite and a couple of kids were playing around the fuse with matches. And there was his invitation to search the house. Was Bernie there? No! If I thought she was I'd have searched the house, even though I believed he might have a half-dozen gunmen parked above. But it wouldn't help Bernie any to have me walk upstairs and get my roof shot off at the top step.

No—I thought it better to fall in with his humour and try to trip him. I'd turn a back flip and take the attitude that after all maybe he was a very wronged man. And I did.

'I only know what I'm told, doctor,' I said brusquely. 'You can't blame me for investigating the girl's story—especially since she disappeared. Now—her mother is dead; did you happen to meet this mother as the attending physician?'

And that was a crack he hadn't expected. I scored again. His face did a few quick colours, but he answered without hesitating.

'I was called in by her physician.'

'And his name?' I pulled out a little pad, like a stage detective.

'Doctor Robinfall.' His eyes were narrowing.

'And who signed the death certificate?'

'Enough!' And now there was no mistaking his attitude. He was rattled; his poise was gone; his long fingers shook. He was a murderer and a crook; it was all written on his evil face. I hadn't had much doubt before, but now I was sure. Oh, I envied the Central Office detective then. The time was right for a signed confession. A police officer's duty is to the law, and he wouldn't need to worry about the girl. My duty was to the girl, and I had to worry about her.

I followed him as he staggered to the hall. And I gave him the final blow as he stood trembling and pointing at the big front door. There was murder in his heart and in his face—but I watched his hands and advised him once to keep his right further from his pocket. He was a loathsome, slimy thing—fear, stark terror, in his face. I had guessed his secret—his first crime, that would connect him with all the others. Protected as a doctor, he had killed Bernie's mother.

'What are you going to do—what are you going to do?' he kept saying over and over as we stood by the door.

'You must produce the girl at my office at six o'clock tonight.'

'And—what of me?'

'If she is safe—and things are satisfactory, you'll have twenty-four hours for a get-away.'

'She'll die—die—die,' he slobbered like a jibbering idiot, 'if you—you get the police.'

But I only smiled over at him.

'At six o'clock,' I told him, as I backed out the door.

'And if I don't?'

'I'll get an order to exhume the body of her mother.' And as I finished, the door closed. But his white face, with the hollow cheeks and the sunken eyes, still stared through the glass. You've got to admit that the old head sometimes works, as well as lead. But I didn't strut, and I didn't pat myself on the back. I'd await results.

Now, my methods are open to criticism, and perhaps some may think I should have stuck to this bird and made him lead me to the girl. And I thought of that, weighed the possibilities, and decided against it. For he was not the only one in this game. There were the two swarthy gentlemen with the trick names, one of whom had croaked Nick. Surely they would have something to say about the girl being turned loose. One of them had committed murder—both of them were in the game deep enough to fry at Sing Sing. Where the dead body would be evidence enough against the doctor, the live Bernie would be evidence against them.

Besides, there was always the possibility of a trap. Of course the girl was not in the house. Doctor Maderia wouldn't know that the girl had never told me his name nor address. He would be expecting me, but he wasn't expecting what I'd bring up about the girl's mother. That was luck. He'd killed her and planned to milk the daughter's bank account dry. It was a pretty game—worthy of a lad with more guts than Doctor Maderia. When the show-down came he blew up. He thought only of himself. My only interest was the girl. The doctor would give his little playmates a story that might bring results.

As for the doctor slipping away on me, he couldn't do it. Two of ˋ the sharpest shadows in New York would be on his heels. He'd soon know that, and feel the fear of the hunted criminal. He'd have to produce the girl. Just a few hours stood between him and the road which leads to the electric chair.

At six o'clock, almost to the dot, he walked into my office. And he was alone—and he was a wreck. I almost felt like taking him for a tour of the country, as a living example that crime doesn't pay.

'You've double-crossed me—you've betrayed me. They are down by the door now. They've been following me.'

'So you wanted to beat it. Where's the girl?'

'Those men are not—police officers?'

'Not a chance.' I shook my head. 'They know nothing about you—just obeying my orders. Now—what of the girl?'

'I couldn't bring her,' he told me. 'Don't—don't,' he cried as I reached for the phone. 'Everything that you accuse me of is true—except that I am but a tool. Ferganses planned things. I had stolen money. I was desperate. I was in debt. The girl is very rich yet. But I will lead you to them—to her. Ferganses' pal, Farro, was in the house when you came. They plan a final coup. It is for me to cash the cheque because I am known at the bank. They will torture her to sign, but I will lead you to the house—to them—to her.'

Could I believe him? Was he a great actor or an awful bust? I'd have to chance it. There was no doubt that the girl was in grave danger. Still, I didn't intend to play any Goldy Locks for the three bears. If this lad would double-cross his friends, he would double-cross me at the last moment. There was just one person he'd play straight with. That was—himself. I knew his kind. Like a prize fighter who is hot stuff when he's winning, but who hollers 'foul' at the first real crack in the breadbasket, such was the doctor. When he was hurt he squawked.

'What's the plan?' I asked him.

'Listen—' He rubbed his hands together. 'I have been most careful. I told them that you suspect, and I told them also that you want the girl. But I saw I was at fault there. And I saw, too, that suspicion was entering their heads. Ferganses I spoke to on the phone. Farro, at my house. To them there is no advantage in giving up the girl. And they tell me to tell you that she dies if you go to the police—but if you let her pay them the money, then she can go.'

'How will they arrange to get the money? The bank will be suspicious of large amounts.' And I eyed him closely.

'That is for me to arrange.' He gulped. 'The bank knows me. I can do it. You think perhaps it is best?'

'No. I don't think perhaps it is best.' I stood over him as he crouched there in the chair. 'The girl goes free tonight—or you burn. You knew that—what else have you planned? What is this idea of leading me to them?'

'That could be done.' He nodded vigorously. 'I am to see them tonight—to get a cheque from the girl. So I could bring you to them. But they are desperate men—you might have to kill Ferganses.'

'That's agreeable,' I told him.

'And me—I go free. You remember your promise. They do not deserve consideration from me. They did not trust me. It was not until the girl saw them that she doubted me. It is their own fault. If they had played the game I would not—'

'That's right.' I agreed with his attempt to tell himself what a real guy he was.

He came to his feet and clutched me by the arm.

'You will not have me arrested? I shall have my chance to leave the country if I do this thing? You are a brave man—you shoot quick. You will come on them from behind. They will fight, and you will kill them.' And he got to rubbing his hands again.

'Where are they keeping the girl?'

'In Jersey. I will lead you to the place—we will drive there together.'

'Just where, in Jersey?'

He smiled, in what he considered a knowing way.

'Just where?' I stretched out a hand and took him by the throat. 'You don't think you can fool me any longer!' And, indeed, I was growing impatient. I thought of Bernie; of her youth; of her childish simplicity; of her bringing-up in a convent, and now being in the hands of those two cut-throats.

'I don't dare tell you yet—because I am afraid you will tell the police. Don't—*don't*!' he screamed, as my fingers closed the tighter about his thin neck. And then, 'I will tell.'

And he did. Just beyond Newark. Did I believe him? I didn't know and I didn't care. I was heartily sick of this detective business. It isn't in my line. What I need is action. What I generally get is action. If it was a trap, all well and good; my guns were loaded and oiled. If it was shooting the boys wanted, they were welcome to it.

Some may question my right—my ethics—in letting him go if I saved the girl. And I'll admit there's room for argument there. But I must play the game as I see it. After all, it's my business and I must run it my own way. Besides, there was the possibility that he wasn't on the level, and I might have to slip a bit of lead into his miserable carcass anyway. And that was a thought worth imparting to the crouching dog who seemed to think of nothing but his own safety.

'You understand the situation thoroughly,' I said to him gravely, for I was not fooling. 'You are to lead me to the girl; you are to lead me so that my coming will be a complete surprise to these pals of yours. You will always be ahead of me—never behind me, and my gun will cover you. You could lead me to a trap where I would be killed. That is possible, but not probable. But it is impossible that you could live. At the first sign of suspicion I'll put a bullet in your back. Don't labour under any delusion that I'm too high-hat and nobleminded to shoot a man in cold blood. You know my record. So—we understand each other.'

His cheeks whitened and his eyes sank the deeper as he nodded, but back in his head might be the hope of betraying me. He felt, maybe, that his time would come. He felt, perhaps, that Ferganses would not be taken alive, and while we shot it out would come his chance. And I smiled to myself. Just before any shooting started the good doctor would be tapped bye-bye with the barrel of my gun. Not a pretty thought, maybe—but, then, I don't go in for pretty thoughts.

As we waited for a later hour to depart the doctor's spirits grew brighter and he began to look on me as his partner, and confided in me. It seems that he didn't trust these other men, anyway, and that he had intended to double-cross them in the long run. From his story they had gotten a few thousand from the girl. It was his idea to take the money in easy stages, but his friends were all for quick action. He didn't exactly tell me that he had killed Bernie's mother—signed the death certificate and framed Bernie in Italy, but he didn't need to. He was all rotten—and more than once he hinted at the pile of jack I could make if I helped him out.

I wasn't mad and I didn't fly at him. I just smiled to myself. If he made a false move and I plugged him, I'd have an easy conscience. Let him think he was a bright boy and encouraged him to go on—and I found out how Nick had gotten his. Nick had been paid earlier in the evening to let the two swarthy lads cart out Bernie. But at that time he knew nothing, and he hadn't suspected I was in the game until he saw one of the Italians lying in the hall. But Nick double-crossed me for the money that was in it then and the blackmail he felt certain would follow. And Nick had run quickly around the corner and seen Doctor Maderia's big car with the doctor in it, with the chloroformed girl and the whozzle-headed lad I had cracked. But Nick hadn't seen the swarthy Ferganses, who had dropped behind for the purpose of seeing if Nick would attempt to follow.

And that part of the story, I guess, was true. Doctor Maderia said that Nick reached for a gun and that there was a fight, and he drove on, picking up Ferganses around the corner later. That was the first time he knew that Nick was dead. Whether there was a fight or not did not matter. Certainly Nick was dead.

They had driven to Jersey, left the girl there with Ferganses, and the doctor had returned to New York with the other lad, called Farro. That was his story—and it was true enough, I guess. At least, as near the truth as would ever come out. But the more the doctor took me into his confidence the more I distrusted him. Was he just trying to make me less cautious—telling me everything, yet telling me nothing that I really didn't know already?

Of course I got Bernie's last name and all about her mother and her father, but why go into that? I would not give her real name, anyway, so we'll just continue to call her Bernie. That I had frisked the doctor and copped all his hardware is hardly necessary to say. But I had.

The doctor was to be at the house in Jersey at one o'clock; Farro had left for the place early in the day. The doctor was booked to start at twelve, so I thought we'd better start at eleven.

'You'll drive,' I told him, as we stepped into the car.

'But I don't know how. I give you my word that I shall make no attempt to—'

'Stick your hands behind your back then,' I said, swinging him around.

'What—what are you going to do?'

'Put the cuffs on you. Come! Make it snappy.'

And that was enough. He didn't fancy having his hands bound behind him, and he learned to drive in jig time.

'I drive a little—but not well,' he stammered.

'I'm not particular—jump in.' I opened the door of the car for him.

And we were off. That was the doctor's first attempt to put it over on me. Or was it? But it didn't matter. I didn't intend this to be a pleasure trip. I was expecting most anything to happen. Bernie was about to receive her delayed service.

Doctor Maderia booked the trip across the Hudson River at Forty-second Street, so I decided to cross at One Hundred and Twenty-fifth. Not that I was just obstinate—but I thought it more conducive to long life and the pursuit of liberty to pick my own route. So we left the ferry at Fort Lee and wound our way up the big hill. And the doctor forgot that he was a novice and drove remarkably well.

But as we shot off towards Newark he got nervous—twice he shifted gears on a hill that a car like mine would race over at forty. There was something on his mind besides his hat, and at length he came out with it.

'Mr Williams,' he said suddenly, paying due respect to my age and dignity with the 'mister', 'I didn't tell you all the truth—the house is not near Newark—rather, up by Englewood.'

'Yes?' I fingered the gun in my lap. 'You're sure this time?'

And he nodded.

'Because,' I went on, 'we must reach the house by twelve o'clock. If we don't—' I shrugged my shoulders. 'Well—Doctor, you'll be a most distressing corpse.'

If it was a joke he missed it, for he was turning the car and we nearly backed into a ditch.

'I am not going to double-cross you,' he gulped. 'I lied because I feared you might break faith with me once you knew the truth, and arrange for the police to come. But now—I shall drive you straight there.'

'You must suit yourself,' I said icily as I snapped out my watch. 'You have until twelve o'clock.' I didn't say any more. I didn't need to; he understood me. And, after all, there was a certain amount of reason for him lying to me at first. I had thought of the police, of course. I never use them if I can help it, but I would use them if I thought it was for the benefit of my client. But here—once the police came into the case—Bernie would go up. Another murder wouldn't bother these lads. Unfortunately, you can only electrocute murderers once.

We passed through Englewood and back towards the Hudson River. There, just at the top of the Palisades, we turned and followed a fairly good highway—shot into a side road and he stopped the car.

'It is only—a few—hundred yards further.' His lips quivered and the words trembled like a popular 'mammy' song.

'You suggest that we walk?' I asked.

'It is best.' He stuck close to me as we left the car. 'This Ferganses—he is a killer. You must shoot without hesitating—in the back, if possible.'

31

'Fine—we'll ask him to turn around, then.' But my levity didn't cheer up the doctor. His legs were trembling in his pants and his teeth chattering. Maybe it was the cold, and again maybe it wasn't. But I stuck my gun in his back, jerked him erect and told him to lead on. So we started. My own safety lay in the doctor's love of life. He was walking with death, and he knew it.

It's funny, too, what an effect a gun has on the physical as well as the moral attitude of a man. When the doctor's feet would sag and his body slink closer to the ground, I'd just press that gun forward and up he'd come again with a sharp jerk.

So we left the little road, and, with the doctor still doing his jack-in-the-box trick to the sudden prods of my gun, we crossed a wooded field, slipped through the busted part of a barbed-wire fence and saw the house.

Bio, black and ominous it loomed in the moonlight. And then a light—a wavering, flickering flash that came from a room in the upper storey. And it was gone almost at once.

And now we were close to the house.

'How do we get in?' I asked.

'We can use a cellar window—unless you want me to go, alone, by the door and trap them into conversation while you enter.'

There was a laugh in that.

'We'll try the cellar window,' I told him. 'Which side is the best?'

'There is one on this side—and one on the other. But the room above the window on this side is where they will be. You cannot see a light because it is heavily shuttered. Both cellar windows will be locked—you'll have to break one.'

'We'll try the other side—lead on, MacDuff.'

He stopped dead as we reached the back of the house.

'I can't—go—another step—with that gun—against my—back.' And his teeth punctuated each word like a buzz-saw.

And, indeed, he seemed in bad shape. Luckily, the grass was soft and deadened his staggering steps. I had only pushed the gun against him for the moral and physical support. Now, if it didn't have that effect any longer—why, all right. I gave him a few inches leeway. It didn't make any difference to me. Lead travelling half a foot wouldn't lose much of its efficiency.

We went on again, the doctor bending—with me close on his trail. We turned the corner of the house and I saw the splash of light. We were nearing a window of which the shade was half up. Rather venturesome that. These lads felt safe in their retreat, or— And I rubbed my chin—the light in the window was not the only light at that minute. There was a little light slipping through the darkness of my mind. I nodded. We were going to get action, I thought.

So we swung towards the lighted window three feet above the ground—he crouching double again, those lean, long arms—the white fingers at the end of them standing out—swinging back and forth. He paused as he reached the window, and turned to me.

'They'll be in there. You can look in if you wish.'

And I was almost startled by the simplicity of the suggestion. While I looked in that window I would stand directly in the splash of light. Of course I couldn't be seen by those inside, but what about someone outside? If I could have been sure that my visit wasn't expected it would be all right. And really, even though the doctor was a charming chap, you could not expect me to put my entire trust in him.

'You look in, and tell me what's going on,' I said, half sarcastically. And I'll admit that I was surprised when he did stretch up and stand plumb in the light. Nothing happened to him either. But I did notice one thing. He had removed his slouch hat before he looked through the window. Just a habit, that? Maybe—then again, maybe not.

'They are there—both of them—and the girl. Now's your chance. We won't have to enter by the cellar. Come—look.' And he was as excited and as interested as a child.

I didn't say anything. Perhaps, after all, the doctor was on the up and up with me. But I took off my hat there in the darkness and, reaching suddenly out, I placed it on the doctor's head.

The hat had hardly landed; my hand was little more than out of the light; the white face of the doctor had no more than half turned in surprise, doubt, and then fear—when it happened. There was the roar of a gun, a choked scream, a hole in a white face—and the doctor pitched forward on his face. The trap had been sprung—and whether it was successful or not depended entirely upon the point of view you take.

Of course the thing was simple enough. A lad hid in the darkness and watched the lighted window. He was not to fire at a bare head, but was to shoot at the first covered one. My little experiment with the hat looked to him as if the heads had changed. He had made a mistake, of course—but life is full of mistakes; and here he was, coming to pay for his. Yep—he was dashing across the darkness towards the lighted window and the figure beneath it. He thought he had hit me. How sweet and simple of him! But then, I have often contended that crooks are like children.

'All right—all right,' he was calling as he came. Certainly he had the confidence of youth. And as he reached the window it opened, and I recognised the swarthy-faced lad, Ferganses; and I plainly saw the big automatic he held in his right hand.

'You got him, eh, Farro?' And there was something in his voice which was not entirely congratulatory. Farro recognised it, but too late. He was in the light of the window and I could just make out his face. Farro never had the chance to lift the gun in his hand—for Ferganses, in the window, fired at once. Without a cry Farro sank down on top of the doctor.

'It is done, eh, doctor?' Ferganses leaned from the window, his blinking eyes trying to get a good picture of me in the darkness. 'But come,' he went on, taking me for the doctor, 'this Williams is dead—this Farro will no longer want a share. We must burn the money out of the girl, for she is obstinate. Come!'

'Come!' was right. He was hanging half out of the window, with the gun dangling in his hand. And I came. I stepped forward and swung my gun through the air. There was a dull thud, and his chin pounded down on the window-sill. He just sprawled there until I dragged him out and dropped him to the grass.

Maybe I should have shot him and been done with it. But I didn't. It wasn't big-heartedness, nor even a hesitancy about taking a human life. I just thought of my own interest. It was better that he should live. There was a mess there beneath the window that couldn't be hidden from a police investigation. They'd need a victim and they might as well have Ferganses. The authorities would identify the doctor, question the girl, and drag me into it anyway. For once I'd face an investigation as innocent as a new-born babe.

But the girl. I found her all right, in the room above, where I had seen the flashlight. Horribly frightened, of course, yet physically all right but for the stiffness from her bound limbs. And—well, what more would you want, unless to have me go out and walk on Ferganses' face?—which little action I had already done when I climbed in the window. After all, Bernie hadn't gotten such bad service.

ARSON PLUS

Dashiell Hammett

*   *   *

Jim Tarr picked up the cigar I rolled across his desk, looked at the band, bit off an end, and reached for a match.

'Three for a buck,' he said. 'You must want me to break a *couple* of laws for you this time.'

I had been doing business with this fat sheriff of Sacramento County for four or five years—ever since I came to the Continental Detective Agency's San Francisco office—and I had never known him to miss an opening for a sour crack; but it didn't mean anything.

'Wrong both times,' I told him. 'I get them for two bits each, and I'm here to do you a favour instead of asking for one. The company that insured Thornburgh's house thinks somebody touched it off.'

'That's right enough, according to the fire department. They tell me the lower part of the house was soaked with gasoline, but the Lord knows how they could tell—there wasn't a stick left standing. I've got McClump working on it, but he hasn't found anything to get excited about yet.'

'What's the layout? All I know is that there was a fire.'

Tarr leaned back in his chair, turned his red face to the ceiling, and bellowed:

'Hey, Mac!'

The pearl push-buttons on his desk are ornaments so far as he is concerned. Deputy sheriffs McHale, McClump and Macklin came to

36

the door together—MacNab apparently wasn't within hearing.

'What's the idea?' the sheriff demanded of McClump. 'Are you carrying a bodyguard around with you?'

The two other deputies, thus informed as to whom 'Mac' referred this time, went back to their cribbage game.

'We got a city slicker here to catch our firebug for us,' Tarr told his deputy. 'But we got to tell him what it's all about first.'

McClump and I had worked together on an express robbery several months before. He's a rangy, tow-headed youngster of twenty-five or six, with all the nerve in the world—and most of the laziness.

'Ain't the Lord good to us?'

He had himself draped across a chair by now—always his first objective when he comes into a room.

'Well, here's how she stands: this fellow Thornburgh's house was a couple miles out of town, on the old county road—and old frame house. About midnight, night before last, Jeff Pringle—the nearest neighbour, a half-mile or so to the east—saw a glare in the sky from over that way, and phoned in the alarm; but by the time the fire wagons got there, there wasn't enough of the house left to bother about. Pringle was the first of the neighbours to get to the house, and the roof had already fallen in then.

'Nobody saw anything suspicious—no strangers hanging around or nothing. Thornburgh's help just managed to save themselves, and that was all. They don't know much about what happened—too scared, I reckon. But they did see Thornburgh at his window just before the fire got him. A fellow here in town—name of Henderson—saw that part of it too. He was driving home from Wayton, and got to the house just before the roof caved in.

'The fire department people say they found signs of gasoline. The Coonses, Thornburgh's help, say they didn't have no gas on the place. So there you are.'

'Thornburgh have any relatives?'

'Yeah. A niece in San Francisco—a Mrs Evelyn Trowbridge. She was up yesterday, but there wasn't nothing she could do, and she couldn't tell us nothing much, so she went home.'

'Where are the servants now?'

'Here in town. Staying at a hotel on I Street. I told 'em to stick around for a few days.'

'Thornburgh own the house?'

'Uh-huh. Bought it from Newning & Weed a couple months ago.'

'You got anything to do this morning?'

'Nothing but this.'

'Good. Let's get out and dig around.'

We found the Coonses in their room at the hotel on I Street. Mr Coons was a small-boned, plump man with the smooth, meaningless face, and the suavity of the typical male house-servant.

His wife was a tall, stringy woman, perhaps five years older than her husband—say, forty—with a mouth and chin that seemed shaped for gossiping. But he did all the talking, while she nodded her agreement to every second or third word.

'We went to work for Mr Thornburgh on the fifteenth of June, I think,' he said, in reply to my first question. 'We came to Sacramento around the first of the month, and put in applications at the Allis Employment Bureau. A couple of weeks later they sent us out to see Mr Thornburgh, and he took us on.'

'Where were you before you came here?'

'In Seattle, sir, with a Mrs Comerford; but the climate there didn't agree with my wife—she has bronchial trouble—so we decided to come to California. We most likely would have stayed in Seattle, though, if Mrs Comerford hadn't given up her house.'

'What do you know about Thornburgh?'

'Very little, sir. He wasn't a talkative gentleman. He hadn't any business that I know of. I think he was a retired seafaring man. He never said he was, but he had that manner and look. He never went out or had anybody in to see him, except his niece once, and he didn't write or get any mail. He had a room next to his bedroom fixed up as a sort of workshop. He spent most of his time in there. I always thought he was working on some kind of invention, but he kept the door locked, and wouldn't let us go near it.'

'Haven't you any idea at all what it was?'

'No, sir. We never heard any hammering or noises from it, and never smelled anything either. And none of his clothes were ever the least bit soiled, even when they were ready to go out to the laundry. They would have been if he had been working on anything like machinery.'

'Was he an old man?'

'He couldn't have been over fifty, sir. He was very erect, and his hair and beard were thick, with no grey hairs.'

'Ever have any trouble with him?'

'Oh, no, sir! He was, if I may say it, a very peculiar gentleman in a way; and he didn't care about anything except having his meals fixed right, having his clothes taken care of—he was very particular about them—and not being disturbed. Except early in the morning and at night, we'd hardly see him all day.'

'Now about the fire. Tell us the whole thing—everything you remember.'

'Well, sir, my wife and I had gone to bed about ten o'clock, our regular time, and had gone to sleep. Our room was on the second floor, in the rear. Some time later—I never did exactly know what time it was—I woke up, coughing. The room was all full of smoke, and my wife was sort of strangling. I jumped up, and dragged her down the back stairs and out the back door, not thinking of anything but getting her out of there.

'When I had her safe in the yard, I thought of Mr Thornburgh, and tried to get back in the house; but the whole first floor was just flames. I ran around front then, to see if he had got out, but didn't see anything of him. The whole yard was as light as day by then. Then I heard him scream—a horrible scream, sir—I can hear it yet! And I looked up at his window—that was the front second-storey room—and saw him there, trying to get out the window. But all the woodwork was burning, and he screamed again and fell back, and right after that the roof over his room fell in.

'There wasn't a ladder or anything that I could have put up to the window for him—there wasn't anything I could have done.

'In the meantime, a gentleman had left his automobile in the road, and come up to where I was standing; but there wasn't anything we could do—the house was burning everywhere and falling in here and there. So we went back to where I had left my wife, and carried her farther away from the fire, and brought her to—she had fainted. And that's all I know about it, sir.'

'Hear any noises earlier that night? Or see anybody hanging around?'

'No, sir.'

'Have any gasoline around the place?'

'No, sir. Mr Thornburgh didn't have a car.'

'No gasoline for cleaning?'

'No, sir, none at all, unless Mr Thornburgh had it in his work-shop. When his clothes needed cleaning, I took them to town, and all his laundry was taken by the grocer's man, when he brought our provisions.'

'Don't know anything that might have some bearing on the fire?'

'No, sir. I was surprised when I heard that somebody had set the house afire. I could hardly believe it. I don't know why anybody should want to do that . . .'

'What do you think of them?' I asked McClump, as we left the hotel.

'They might pad the bills, or even go South with some of the silver, but they don't figure as killers in my mind.'

That was my opinion, too; but they were the only persons known to have been there when the fire started except the man who had died. We went around to the Allis Employment Bureau and talked to the manager.

He told us that the Coonses had come into his office on June second, looking for work; and had given Mrs Edward Comerford, 45 Woodmansee Terrace, Seattle, Washington, as reference. In reply to a letter—he always checked up the references of servants—Mrs Comerford had written that the Coonses had been in her employ for a number of years, and had been 'extremely satisfactory in every respect.' On June thirteenth, Thornburgh had telephoned the bureau, asking that a man and his wife be sent out to keep house for him, and Allis sent out two couples he had listed. Neither couple had been employed by Thornburgh, though Allis considered them more desirable than the Coonses, who were finally hired by Thornburgh.

All that would certainly seem to indicate that the Coonses hadn't deliberately manoeuvred themselves into the place, unless they were the luckiest people in the world—and a detective can't afford to believe in luck or coincidence, unless he has unquestionable proof of it.

At the office of the real-estate agents, through whom Thornburgh had bought the house—Newning & Weed—we were told that Thornburgh had come in on the eleventh of June, and had said that he had been told that the house was for sale, had looked it over, and wanted to know the price. The deal had been closed the next morning, and he had paid for the house with a cheque for $14,500 on the Seamen's Bank of San Francisco. The house was already furnished.

After luncheon, McClump and I called on Howard Henderson—the man who had seen the fire while driving home from Wayton. He had an office in the Empire Building, with his name and the title *Northern California Agent for Krispy Korn Krumbs* on the door. He was a big, careless-looking man of forty-five or so, with the professionally jovial smile that belongs to the travelling salesman.

He had been in Wayton on business the day of the fire, he said, and had stayed there until rather late, going to dinner and afterwards playing pool with a grocer named Hammersmith—one of his customers. He had left Wayton in his machine, at about ten-thirty, and set out for Sacramento. At Tavender he had stopped at the garage for oil and gas, and to have one of his tyres blown up.

Just as he was about to leave the garage, the garage man had called his attention to a red glare in the sky, and had told him that it was probably from a fire somewhere along the old county road that paralleled the State Road into Sacramento; so Henderson had taken the county road, and had arrived at the burning house just in time to see Thornburgh try to fight his way through the flames.

It was too late to make any attempt to put out the fire, and the man upstairs was beyond saving by then—undoubtedly dead even before the roof collapsed; so Henderson had helped Coons revive his wife, and stayed there watching the fire until it had burned itself out. He had seen no one on that county road while driving to the fire . . .

'What do you know about Henderson?' I asked McClump, when we were on the street.

'Came here, from somewhere in the East, I think, early in the summer to open that breakfast cereal agency. Lives at the Garden Hotel. Where do we go next?'

'We get a car, and take a look at what's left of the Thornburgh house.'

An enterprising incendiary couldn't have found a lovelier spot in which to turn himself loose, if he looked the whole county over. Tree-topped hills hid it from the rest of the world, on three sides; while away from the fourth, an uninhabited plain rolled down to the river. The county road that passed the front gate was shunned by automobiles, so McClump said, in favour of the State Highway to the north.

Where the house had been was now a mound of blackened ruins. We poked around in the ashes for a few minutes—not that we expected to find anything, but because it's the nature of man to poke around in ruins.

A garage in the rear, whose interior gave no evidence of recent occupation, had a badly scorched roof and front, but was otherwise undamaged. A shed behind it, sheltering an axe, a shovel, and various odds and ends of gardening tools, had escaped the fire altogether. The lawn in front of the house, and the garden behind the shed—about an acre in all—had been pretty thoroughly cut and trampled by wagon wheels, and the feet of the firemen and the spectators.

Having ruined our shoe-shines, McClump and I got back in our car and swung off in a circle around the place, calling at all the houses within a mile radius, and getting little besides jolts for our trouble.

The nearest house was that of Pringle, the man who had turned in the alarm; but he not only knew nothing about the dead man, he said he had never even seen him. In fact, only one of the neighbours had ever seen him: a Mrs Jabine, who lived about a mile to the south.

She had taken care of the key to the house while it was vacant; and a day or two before he bought it, Thornburgh had come to her house, enquiring about the vacant one. She had gone over there with him and shown him through it, and he had told her that he intended buying it, if the price, of which neither of them knew anything, wasn't too high.

He had been alone, except for the chauffeur of the hired car in which he had come from Sacramento, and, save that he had no family, he had told her nothing about himself.

Hearing that he had moved in, she went over to call on him several days later—'just a neighbourly visit'—but had been told by Mrs Coons that he was not at home. Most of the neighbours had talked to the Coonses, and had got the impression that Thornburgh did not care for visitors, so they had let him alone. The Coonses were described as 'pleasant enough to talk to when you meet them', but reflecting their employer's desire not to make friends.

McClump summarised what the afternoon had taught us as we pointed our car towards Tavender: 'Any of these folks could have touched off the place, but we got nothing to show that any of 'em even knew Thornburgh, let alone had a bone to pick with him.'

Tavender turned out to be a crossroads settlement of a general store and post office, a garage, a church, and six dwellings, about two miles from Thornburgh's place. McClump knew the storekeeper and postmaster, a scrawny little man named Philo, who stuttered moistly.

'I n-n-never s-saw Th-thornburgh,' he said, 'and I n-n-never had any m-mail for him. C-coons'—it sounded like one of these things butterflies come out of—'used to c-come in once a week t-to order groceries—they d-didn't have a phone. He used to walk in, and I'd s-send the stuff over in my c-c-car. Th-then I'd s-see him once in a while, waiting f-for the stage to S-s-sacramento.'

'Who drove the stuff out to Thornburgh's?'

'M-m-my b-boy. Want to t-talk to him?'

The boy was a juvenile edition of the old man, but without the stutter.

He had never seen Thornburgh on any of his visits, but his business had taken him only as far as the kitchen. He hadn't noticed anything peculiar about the place.

'Who's the night man at the garage?' I asked him.

'Billy Luce. I think you can catch him there now. I saw him go in a few minutes ago.'

We crossed the road and found Luce.

'Night before last—the night of the fire down the road—was there a man here talking to you when you first saw it?'

He turned his eyes upward in that vacant stare which people use to aid their memory.

'Yes, I remember now! He was going to town, and I told him that if he took the county road instead of the State Road he'd see the fire on his way in.'

'What kind of looking man was he?'

'Middle-aged—a big man, but sort of slouchy. I think he had on a brown suit, baggy and wrinkled.'

'Medium complexion?'

'Yes.'

'Smile when he talked?'

'Yes, a pleasant sort of fellow.'

'Brown hair?'

'Yeah, but have a heart!' Luce laughed. 'I didn't put him under a magnifying glass.'

From Tavender we drove over to Wayton. Luce's description had fit Henderson all right, but while we were at it, we thought we might as well check up to make sure that he had been coming from Wayton.

We spent exactly twenty-five minutes in Wayton; ten of them finding Hammersmith, the grocer with whom Henderson had said he dined and played pool; five minutes finding the proprietor of the pool room; and ten verifying Henderson's story . . .

'What do you think of it now, Mac?' I asked, as we rolled back towards Sacramento.

Mac's too lazy to express an opinion, or even form one, unless he's driven to it; but that doesn't mean they aren't worth listening to.

'There ain't a hell of a lot to think,' he said cheerfully. 'Henderson is out of it, if he ever was in it. There's nothing to show that anybody but the Coonses and Thornburgh were there when the fire started—but there may have been a regiment there. Them Coonses ain't too honest-looking, maybe, but they ain't killers, or I miss my guess. But

43

the fact remains that they're the only bet we got so far. Maybe we ought to try to get a line on them.'

'All right,' I agreed. 'Soon as we get back to town, I'll get a wire off to our Seattle office asking them to interview Mrs Comerford, and see what she can tell about them. Then I'm going to catch a train for San Francisco and see Thornburgh's niece in the morning.'

Next morning, at the address McClump had given me—a rather elaborate apartment building on California Street—I had to wait three-quarters of an hour for Mrs Evelyn Trowbridge to dress. If I had been younger, or a social caller, I suppose I'd have felt amply rewarded when she finally came in—a tall, slender woman of less than thirty; in some sort of clinging black affair; with a lot of black hair over a very white face, strikingly set off by a small red mouth and big hazel eyes that looked black until you got close to them.

But I was a busy, middle-aged detective, who was fuming over having his time wasted; and I was a lot more interested in finding the bird who struck the match than I was in feminine beauty. However, I smothered my grouch, apologised for disturbing her at such an early hour, and got down to business.

'I want you to tell me all you know about your uncle—his family, friends, enemies, business connections—everything.'

I had scribbled on the back of the card I had sent in to her what my business was.

'He hadn't any family,' she said; 'unless I might be it. He was my mother's brother, and I am the only one of that family now living.'

'Where was he born?'

'Here in San Francisco. I don't know the date, but he was about fifty years old, I think—three years older than my mother.'

'What was his business?'

'He went to sea when he was a boy, and, so far as I know, always followed it until a few months ago.'

'Captain?'

'I don't know. Sometimes I wouldn't see or hear from him for several years, and he never talked about what he was doing; though he would mention some of the places he had visited—Rio de Janeiro, Madagascar, Tobago, Christiania. Then, about three months ago—some time in May—he came here and told me that he was through with wandering; that he was going to take a house in some quiet place where he could work undisturbed on an invention in which he was interested.

'He lived at the Francisco Hotel while he was in San Francisco. After a couple of weeks he suddenly disappeared. And then, about a month ago, I received a telegram from him, asking me to come to see him at his house near Sacramento. I went up the very next day, and I thought that he was acting queerly—he seemed very excited over something. He gave me a will that he had just drawn up and some life insurance policies in which I was beneficiary.

'Immediately after that he insisted that I return home, and hinted rather plainly that he did not wish me to either visit him again or write until I heard from him. I thought all that rather peculiar, as he had always seemed fond of me. I never saw him again.'

'What was this invention he was working on?'

'I really don't know. I asked him once, but he became so excited—even suspicious—that I changed the subject, and never mentioned it again.'

'Are you sure that he really did follow the sea all those years?'

'No, I am not. I just took it for granted; but he may have been doing something altogether different.'

'Was he ever married?'

'Not that I know of.'

'Know any of his friends or enemies?'

'No, none.'

'Remember anybody's name that he ever mentioned?'

'No.'

'I don't want you to think this next question insulting, though I admit it is. But it has to be asked. Where were you on the night of the fire?'

'At home; I had some friends here to dinner, and they stayed until about midnight. Mr and Mrs Walker Kellogg, Mrs John Dupree, and a Mr Killmer, who is a lawyer. I can give you their addresses, or you can get them from the phone book, if you want to question them.'

From Mrs Trowbridge's apartment I went to the Francisco Hotel. Thornburgh had been registered there from May tenth to June thirteenth, and hadn't attracted much attention. He had been a tall, broad-shouldered, erect man of about fifty, with rather long brown hair brushed straight back; a short, pointed, brown beard, and healthy, ruddy complexion—grave, quiet, punctilious in dress and manner; his hours had been regular and he had had no visitors that any of the hotel employees remembered.

At the Seamen's Bank—upon which Thornburgh's cheque, in payment of the house, had been drawn—I was told that he had opened an

45

account there on May fifteenth, having been introduced by W. W. Jeffers & Sons, local stock brokers. A balance of a little more than four hundred dollars remained to his credit. The cancelled cheques on hand were all to the order of various life insurance companies; and for amounts that, if they represented premiums, testified to rather large policies. I jotted down the names of the life insurance companies, and then went to the office of W. W. Jeffers & Sons.

Thornburgh had come in, I was told, on the tenth of May with $15,000 worth of bonds that he wanted sold. During one of his conversations with Jeffers he had asked the broker to recommend a bank, and Jeffers had given him a letter to the Seamen's Bank.

That was all Jeffers knew about him. He gave me the numbers of the bonds, but tracing bonds isn't always the easiest thing in the world.

The reply to my Seattle telegram was waiting for me at the Continental Detective Agency when I arrived.

MRS EDWARD COMERFORD RENTED APARTMENT AT ADDRESS YOU GIVE ON MAY TWENTY-FIVE. GAVE IT UP JUNE SIX. TRUNKS TO SAN FRANCISCO SAME DAY. CHECK NUMBERS GN FOUR FIVE TWO FIVE EIGHT SEVEN AND EIGHT AND NINE

Tracing baggage is no trick at all, if you have the dates and check numbers to start with—as many a bird who is wearing somewhat similar numbers on his chest and back, because he overlooked that detail when making his getaway, can tell you—and twenty-five minutes in a baggage-room at the ferry and half an hour in the office of a transfer company gave me my answer.

The trunks had been delivered to Mrs Evelyn Trowbridge's apartment!

I got Jim Tarr on the phone.

'Good shooting!' he said, forgetting for once to indulge his wit. 'We'll grab the Coonses here and Mrs Trowbridge there, and that's the end of another mystery.'

'Wait a minute!' I cautioned him. 'It's not all straightened out yet—there's still a few kinks in the plot.'

'It's straight enough for me. I'm satisfied.'

'You're the boss, but I think you're being a little hasty. I'm going up to talk with the niece again. Give me a little time before you phone the police here to make the pinch. I'll hold her until they get there.'

*

Evelyn Trowbridge let me in this time, instead of the maid who had opened the door for me in the morning, and she led me to the same room in which we had had our first talk. I let her pick out a seat, and then I selected one that was closer to either door than hers was.

On the way up I had planned a lot of innocent-sounding questions that would get her all snarled up; but after taking a good look at this woman sitting in front of me, leaning comfortably back in her chair, coolly waiting for me to speak my piece, I discarded the trick stuff and came out cold-turkey.

'Ever use the name Mrs Edward Comerford?'

'Oh, yes.' As casual as a nod on the street.

'When?'

'Often. You see, I happen to have been married not so long ago to Mr Edward Comerford. So it's not really strange that I should have used the name.'

'Use it in Seattle recently?'

'I would suggest,' she said sweetly, 'that if you are leading up to the references I gave Coons and his wife, you might save time by coming right to it?'

'That's fair enough,' I said. 'Let's do that.'

There wasn't a tone or shading, in voice, manner, or expression, to indicate that she was talking about anything half so serious or important to her as a possibility of being charged with murder. She might have been talking about the weather, or a book that hadn't interested her particularly.

'During the time that Mr Comerford and I were married, we lived in Seattle, where he still lives. After the divorce, I left Seattle and resumed my maiden name. And the Coonses *were* in our employ, as you might learn if you care to look it up. You'll find my husband—or former husband—at the Chelsea apartments.

'Last summer, or late spring, I decided to return to Seattle. The truth of it is—I suppose all my personal affairs will be aired anyhow—that I thought perhaps Edward and I might patch up our differences; so I went back and took an apartment on Woodmansee Terrace. As I was known in Seattle as Mrs Edward Comerford, and as I thought my using his name might influence him a little, I used it while I was there.

'Also I telephoned the Coonses to make tentative arrangements in case Edward and I should open our house again; but Coons told me that they were going to California, and so I gladly gave them an excellent recommendation when, some days later, I received a letter of enquiry from an employment bureau in Sacramento. After I had been in Seattle for about two weeks, I changed my mind about the reconciliation—Edward's interest, I learned, was all centred elsewhere; so I returned to San Francisco—'

'Very nice! But—'

'If you will permit me to finish,' she interrupted. 'When I went to see my uncle in response to his telegram, I was surprised to find the Coonses in his house. Knowing my uncle's peculiarities, and finding them now increased, and remembering his extreme secretiveness about his mysterious invention, I cautioned the Coonses not to tell him that they had been in my employ.

'He certainly would have discharged them, and just as certainly would have quarrelled with me—he would have thought that I was having him spied on. Then, when Coons telephoned me after the fire, I knew that to admit that the Coonses had been formerly in my employ would, in view of the fact that I was my uncle's only heir, cast suspicion on all three of us. So we foolishly agreed to say nothing about it and carry on the deception.'

That didn't sound all wrong—but it didn't sound all right. I wished Tarr had taken it easier and let us get a better line on these people, before having them thrown in the coop.

'The coincidence of the Coonses stumbling into my uncle's house is, I fancy, too much for your detecting instincts,' she went on, as I didn't say anything. 'Am I to consider myself under arrest?'

I'm beginning to like this girl; she's a nice, cool piece of work.

'Not yet,' I told her. 'But I'm afraid it's going to happen pretty soon.'

She smiled a little mocking smile at that, and another when the doorbell rang.

It was O'Hara from police headquarters. We turned the apartment upside down and inside out, but didn't find anything of importance except the will she had told me about, dated July eighth, and her uncle's life insurance policies. They were all dated between May fifteenth and June tenth, and added up to a little more than $200,000.

I spent an hour grilling the maid after O'Hara had taken Evelyn Trowbridge away, but she didn't know any more than I did. However, between her, the janitor, the manager of the apartments, and the names Mrs Trowbridge had given me, I learned that she had really been entertaining friends on the night of the fire—until after eleven o'clock, anyway—and that was late enough.

Half an hour later I was riding the Short Line back to Sacramento.

I was getting to be one of the line's best customers, and my anatomy was on bouncing terms with every bump in the road!

Between bumps I tried to fit the pieces of this Thornburgh puzzle together. The niece and the Coonses fitted in somewhere, but not just where we had them. We had been working on the job sort of lopsided, but it was the best we could do with it. In the beginning we had turned to the Coonses and Evelyn Trowbridge because there was no other direction to go; and now we had something on them—but a good lawyer could make hash out of it.

The Coonses were in the county jail when I got to Sacramento. After some questioning they had admitted their connection with the niece, and had come through with stories that matched hers in every detail.

Tarr, McClump and I sat around the sheriff's desk and argued.

'Those yarns are pipe dreams,' the sheriff said. 'We got all three of 'em cold, and there's nothing else to it. They're as good as convicted.'

McClump grinned derisively at his superior, and then turned to me.

'Go on, you tell him about the holes in his little case. He ain't your boss, and can't take it out on you later for being smarter than he is!'

Tarr glared from one of us to the other.

'Spill it, you wise guys!' he ordered.

'Our dope is,' I told him, figuring that McClump's view of it was the same as mine, 'that there's nothing to show that even Thornburgh knew he was going to buy that house before the tenth of June, and that the Coonses were in town looking for work on the second. And besides, it was only by luck that they got the jobs. The employment office sent two couples out there ahead of them.'

'We'll take a chance on letting the jury figure that out.'

'Yes? You'll also take a chance on them figuring out that Thornburgh, who seems to have been a nut, might have touched off the place himself! We've got something on these people, Jim, but not enough to go into court with them. How are you going to prove that when the Coonses were planted in Thornburgh's house—if you can even prove that they and the Trowbridge woman knew he was going to load up with insurance policies?'

The sheriff spat disgustedly.

'You guys are the limit! You run around in circles, digging up the dope on these people until you get enough to hang 'em, and then you run around hunting for outs! What's the matter with you now?'

I answered him from halfway to the door—the pieces were beginning to fit together under my skull.

'Going to run some more circles—come on, Mac!'

McClump and I held a conference on the fly, and then I got a car from the nearest garage and headed for Tavender. We made time going out, and got there before the general store had closed for the night. The stuttering Philo separated himself from the two men with whom he had been talking, and followed me to the rear of the store.

'Do you keep an itemised list of the laundry you handle?'

'N-n-no; just the amounts.'

'Let's look at Thornburgh's.'

He produced a begrimed and rumpled account book, and we picked out the weekly items I wanted: $2.60, $3.10, $2.25, and so on.

'Got the last batch of laundry here?'

'Y-yes,' he said. 'It j-just c-c-came out from the city t-today.'

I tore open the bundle—some sheets, pillowcases, tablecloths, towels, napkins; some feminine clothing; some shirts, collars, underwear, and socks that were unmistakably Coons's. I thanked Philo while running back to the car.

Back in Sacramento again, McClump was waiting for me at the garage where I had hired the car.

'Registered at the hotel on June fifteenth, rented the office on the sixteenth. I think he's in the hotel now,' he greeted me.

We hurried around the block to the Garden Hotel.

'Mr Henderson went out a minute or two ago,' the night clerk told us. 'He seemed to be in a hurry.'

'Know where he keeps his car?'

'In the hotel garage around the corner.'

We were within ten feet of the garage, when Henderson's automobile shot out and turned up the street.

'Oh, Mr Henderson!' I cried, trying to keep my voice level.

He stepped on the gas and streaked away from us.

'Want him?' McClump asked; and at my nod he stopped a passing roadster by the simple expedient of stepping in front of it.

We climbed in, McClump flashed his star at the bewildered driver, and pointed out Henderson's dwindling tail-light. After he had persuaded himself that he wasn't being boarded by a couple of bandits, the commandeered driver did his best, and we picked up Henderson's tail-light after two or three turnings, and closed in on him—though his car was going at a good clip.

By the time we reached the outskirts of the city, we had crawled up to within safe shooting distance, and I sent a bullet over the fleeing man's head. Thus encouraged, he managed to get a little more speed out of his car; but we were definitely overhauling him now.

Just at the wrong minute Henderson decided to look over his shoulder at us—an unevenness in the road twisted his wheels—his machine swayed—skidded—went over on its side. Almost immediately, from the heart of the tangle, came a flash and a bullet moaned past my ear. Another. And then, while I was still hunting for something to shoot at in the pile of junk we were drawing down upon, McClump's ancient and battered revolver roared in my other ear.

Henderson was dead when we got to him—McClump's bullet had taken him over one eye.

McClump said over the body:

'I ain't an inquisitive sort of fellow, but I hope you don't mind telling me why I shot this lad.'

'Because he was—*Thornburgh*.'

He didn't say anything for about five minutes. Then: 'I reckon that's right. How'd you know it?'

We were sitting beside the wreckage now, waiting for the police that we had sent our commandeered chauffeur to phone for.

'He had to be,' I said, 'when you think it all over. Funny we didn't hit on it before! All that stuff we were told about Thornburgh had a fishy sound. Whiskers and an unknown profession, immaculate and working on a mysterious invention, very secretive and born in San Francisco—where the fire wiped out all the old records—just the sort of fake that could be cooked up easily.

'Now, consider Henderson. You had told me he came to Sacramento sometime early this summer—and the dates you got tonight show that he didn't come until *after* Thornburgh had bought his house. All right! Now compare Henderson with the descriptions we got of Thornburgh.

'Both are about the same size and age, and with the same colour hair. The differences are all things that can be manufactured—clothes, a little sunburn, and a month's growth of beard, along with a little acting, would do the trick. Tonight I went out to Tavender and took a look at the last batch of laundry—*and there wasn't any that didn't fit the Coonses!* And none of the bills all the way back were large enough for Thornburgh to have been as careful about his clothes as we were told he was.'

'It must be great to be a detective!' McClump grinned as the police ambulance came up and began disgorging policemen. 'I reckon somebody must have tipped Henderson off that I was asking about him this evening.' And then, regretfully: 'So we ain't going to hang them folks for murder after all.'

'No, but we oughtn't have any trouble convicting them of arson plus conspiracy to defraud, and anything else that the Prosecuting Attorney can think up.'

DEAD MAN'S HEAD

Robert Leslie Bellem

*   *   *

I opened the package and a human head rolled out into my lap. A man's head—with a bullet-hole between the eyes.

It was late at night, in my apartment. I'd been to see Chaplin's latest picture at the Chinese, and when I got home I found a bundle wrapped in brown paper outside the door of my flat. I picked it up and carried it in.

There weren't any postage stamps on it; no express-tags, either. Evidently someone had delivered it personally. Printed across the front was: 'For Dan Turner, private detective'. That was all. No sender's name; no return address.

I cut the strings and unwrapped the bundle. And that's when the severed head rolled spang into my lap.

It startled hell out of me. I said: 'What the hell!' and jumped to my feet. The head hit the floor with a gruesome bounce. It rolled halfway across my living-room rug. Then it came to rest, face upward. A damned nasty sight.

For a minute I was shaky as hell. I reached for a bottle of Vat 69 and tilted it down my throat. That made me feel a little better, but not much. I walked over and picked up the severed head.

There wasn't any blood around the bullet-wound in its forehead. None at the neck, either. That had all been washed away, nice and clean. I took one good gander at the white, cold features; and I recognised the face right away.

It was the head of Skinny Arkle. Maybe you remember him. He was a big-shot screen comedian back in the silent days. Skinny Arkle had been even funnier than his name. He'd been tops in the old pie-throwing class, and the way he used to pop his false teeth out of his mouth and fold up his face kept the whole country in stitches. But at the height of his popularity, Skinny Arkle had got himself in a hell of a jam.

He'd gone on a binge in San Diego with an obscure extra dame named Nancy Norward. He and the Norward girl had got plastered together—and the dame kicked the bucket. They'd tried to pin her death on Skinny Arkle, but a jury finally decided she'd cashed in from acute alcoholism coupled with gizzard trouble or something. Anyhow, they turned Skinny loose.

Just the same, the scandal had cooked Skinny Arkle's goose in the movies. All the studios blacklisted him; the stink had given Hollywood too much of a black eye, so Skinny had to take the rap—be the goat.

He'd faded out of pictures; hadn't appeared in a single film since the mess. For a while he went back to his native Jugoslavia; then he returned to Hollywood and married a cute kid named Kitty Calvert—a wren with red hair and a shape like seven million bucks. She was an Alta-mount semi-star, and she dragged down enough cookies in her weekly pay-envelope to keep herself and Skinny well fixed. For that matter, it was rumoured that Skinny himself had salted away a nice stack of geetus from the days when he was in the big dough.

Well, that was Skinny Arkle's history as I remembered it. And now, here was his decapitated head grinning at me from my living-room floor—with a bullet-hole in its brain.

I picked up the head and put it on my library table. Then I grabbed for my phone. I dialled the home number of my friend, Dave Donaldson of the homicide squad. When he answered, I said: 'This is Dan Turner. Listen, Dave—something screwy has happened.' I told him.

Dave said: 'For God's sake! Say—you're not drunk, are you? You haven't got pink elephants, have you?'

'Hell, no. This is on the level,' I told him.

He said: 'Cripes! Meet me down at headquarters in fifteen minutes. Bring that head with you!'

I said: 'Okay,' and hung up. Then all of a sudden I thought I heard a sound outside my door.

I was nervous anyhow. I had the jitters. I dragged out the .32 automatic I always carry in a shoulder-holster, and I dived for the door.

There was a tall, statuesque blonde bimbo standing outside my door for some while. She looked scared as hell when I popped out at her. She said: 'Oh-h-h—!' in a sort of muffled gasp.

I said: 'Who the hell are you? What do you want?'

'I—I'm looking for Dan Turner,' she answered me.

I looked her over. She seemed worried, all right. But she was gorgeous, too—in a flashy sort of way. Her blonde head came above my shoulder, and I'm over six-feet-two. At a guess, I'd say she was close to thirty—but she wore a damned good make-up that made her look younger. And her figure was something to remember.

She wasn't skinny, like a lot of tall dames. She wasn't too hefty, either. Just well-proportioned for her size. Sleek and slinky! Every lithe contour, every curve exactly right.

I said: 'Well, kiddo, I'm sorry you're worried, but I haven't got time to talk to you now. See me at my office tomorrow.'

She said: 'No! You've got to listen to me right now, Mr Turner! You must!'

I thought of my date with Donaldson at headquarters in fifteen minutes. I said: 'Sorry, sister. You'll have to excuse me.'

'You—you mean you won't listen to me?'

'Sure I'll listen to you. Tomorrow.'

Her eyes got sort of wild-looking. She said: 'I'll *make* you listen!' And before I could stop her she rumpled up her yellow hair and ripped at the front of her dress. She said: 'I'll scream and tell people you attacked me!'

'Hell!' I said. 'If it's that important, go ahead and spill your story. But cover yourself up or maybe you'll have something to scream about.'

I reached over and pulled her frock together. My fingers were tingling at the near contact.

The girl said: 'I—I'm Constance Calvert. I'm Kitty Calvert's sister. Kitty Calvert, the Altamount star. She's Skinny Arkle's wife.'

I stiffened. 'Yeah?'

'Yes. And I'm worried for Kitty. Afraid for her. Skinny Arkle and she have had a terrible row. Skinny left after the fight. That was three days ago. He left, threatening to come back and m-murder Kitty. We haven't seen him since, but I'm frightened. I want you to find him—'

I grabbed her by the arm and said: 'Come on in my apartment. I want to show you something. You won't have to worry about Skinny Arkle any more.'

I pulled her into my living-room. She saw Skinny Arkle's severed head on my table. She went white. 'Oh, my God!' she choked. And then damn' if she didn't faint!

She fell sprawling on the floor, and the torn front of her dress gaped open. White skin peeped from the ripped frock.

I said: 'What the hell—!' and leaned over her, lifted her up. I carried her into the next room, put her on the divan. She was dead to the world. I didn't know how long it would take me to bring her round—but I didn't have time, just then. I had to scram down to headquarters to keep my date with Donaldson.

On the other hand it struck me that this blonde baby, Constance Calvert, might be a key to the whole business.

It was stretching the long leg of coincidence to think she had just accidentally come to me the same night I'd received Arkle's decapitated noggin. She was mixed up in the deal some way. Maybe she was the one who'd brought that package and left it at my door!

Well, I couldn't take her down to headquarters with me. Not when she was unconscious. But I didn't want her to get away. So I used a trick I'd pulled many a time before.

I stripped the dress off her limp form, and took her shoes and chiffon stockings off while I was at it. The whole business got me hot under the collar. But I stuck to my job and pretty soon I had her down to black lace underthings.

She was a hell of a sweet number. Her skin was as smooth and warm as new cream, and she had what it takes to drive a man utsnay. But I didn't have time to be driven utsnay, so I covered her with a blanket and left her.

I carried her duds out with me. I picked up Skinny's head, wrapped it in the brown paper, and went down to my jalopy. Then I drove to beat hell.

Dave Donaldson was waiting outside headquarters. We went into his office and I showed him the head. He said: 'For Cripes' sake! It's Arkle, all right. Now, who in hell—?'

I said: 'Wait a minute. Don't pop off with a lot of screwy questions. Don't ask me why this damned thing was delivered to my apartment. That's one goofy thing I don't pretend to understand. But I've got a theory about Skinny Arkle's death.'

Donaldson said: 'A theory?'

'Yes. Now listen. Arkle was married to a girl named Kitty Calvert. Kitty has a sister, Constance Calvert. Well, just as I was starting downtown to meet you, Constance came to my door. She's a tall, blonde bimbo with plenty of sex-appeal.'

'The hell with that,' Donaldson grunted. 'What did she want?'

'She claimed she was scared for her sister,' I said. 'She said Kitty and Skinny Arkle had a hell of a row three days ago. Skinny threatened Kitty's life. Then he took it on the lam and hasn't been seen since.'

'So what?' Donaldson rasped.

'So this. Maybe Constance Calvert's story was a frame-up. Maybe her sister did have a fight with Skinny; and maybe Kitty shot the poor devil. Then maybe Kitty sent her sister to see me.'

'What for?'

I said: 'To cover the murder. To make it look as if they didn't know where Skinny had gone to.'

Donaldson said: 'Where is Kitty Calvert's sister now?'

'In my apartment. She won't get away.'

He said: 'Wait till I turn this head over to the medical examiner. Then we'll go see Kitty.'

He was gone about two minutes. Then we went out and piled into my jalopy. I drove—and I didn't spare the speedometer. Pretty soon we parked outside the Arkle home in Westwood.

I noticed another machine standing at the kerb a couple of doors away. It was a big, shiny maroon Cad, and somehow I thought I recognised it. But I couldn't be sure, and there was no point in checking it up just then. Donaldson and I went up to the porch of the Arkle house and rang the bell.

A cute little Chink maid opened up. I said: 'We want to see Mrs Arkle, please.'

The Chink maid spoke perfect English. American-born, probably. She said: 'Miss Kitty Calvert has retired, sir. You'll have to come in the morning.'

Dave Donaldson shoved me aside and flashed his badge. 'We'll see her now!' he growled.

The maid widened her slanted eyes. 'But—there's someone with—' she started to say. Then she stopped and blushed a little.

I said: 'Somebody with her, eh? A man?'

'I—don't know anything about it, sir,' the Chink dame said. I could tell she was lying. Her left hand sort of fluttered towards her heart, covering her breast through her uniform.

Donaldson didn't waste any more time. He pushed the Oriental girl aside and said: 'Come on, Turner.' He ran up the stairs. I followed him. And then, just as we reached the second floor, I heard a shot.

I said: 'What the hell—!' and made a dive for a closed door. The shot had sounded from within the room beyond that door. I jammed into it with my shoulder, burst it open. I had my .32 automatic in my fist. I leaped into the room, with Donaldson at my heels.

The room was all done in pink, with a pink-shaded lamp glowing in one corner. I sniffed the scent of expensive perfume. But I smelled something else, too. It was the acrid odour of powder-smoke.

In one second I caught the whole scene. There on the bed lay an almost nude woman—a girl. A girl with red hair and the prettiest figure I ever saw; the prettiest legs. An absolute knockout. It was Kitty Calvert—Skinny Arkle's wife.

She was as dead as a smoked fish.

There was a bullet-hole in her breast, right over the heart. She'd been shot plumb centre. And where she was shot there was a round red hole, with blood seeping out of it.

Directly beyond the bed I saw a man standing. He had his coat and vest off, and he looked white as hell. And he had a roscoe in his mitt.

I recognised him. He was Billy Sanston—a big-shot director for Alta-mount Studios. In fact, he directed all Kitty Calvert's productions. And now I knew where I'd seen that maroon Cad before—the one that was parked downstairs. It was Sanston's own Cad. I'd seen him driving it many a time.

Donaldson said: 'You murdering rat!' and took aim at Sanston. 'Drop that gun, you louse!'

Sanston dropped the gun. It hit the floor. He said: 'Good God—you don't think I—?'

Donaldson said: 'I don't think anything. If you've got anything to say, save it for your lawyer. Stick out your fins for the nippers.'

The movie director staggered a little. 'But—but you can't arrest me for something I didn't do! My God, I'll be ruined! My wife will divorce me—I'll lose my job—'

'You should have thought of that before. You been playing around with Kitty Calvert, haven't you?'

Sanston flushed. 'Y-yes, but I didn't kill her; I swear I didn't! I was here with her tonight. I admit that. I—I just went into the next room for a minute. Then I heard a shot. I ran in here and saw Kitty on the bed. She was dead; the gun was beside her. I—I picked it up, and then you men broke in. She—she must have shot herself—'

'Nuts!' Donaldson growled. 'Come on—or shall I sock you on the dome with the soft end of my roscoe?'

Sanston swayed towards us, holding out his hands for the bracelets. Then he pulled an unexpected stunt. With his left he smashed Dave Donaldson's service .38 aside. Then he planted a haymaker on Donaldson's jaw. Dave went down.

I leaped at Sanston, but he got away from me. He scooped up the gat he had dropped. I drew a bead on him, pulled my trigger. But like a damn' fool I'd forgotten to unlatch the safety on my automatic. When I squeezed the trigger, nothing happened.

And by that time, Billy Sanston was out of the room and pelting hell-for-leather down the stairs.

I hurled myself after him. Behind me I heard Donaldson getting on his feet. Dave was cursing and staggering along in my trail. I hit the stairs, started down. But Sanston had a good start. Before I was halfway down, I heard the front door slam shut. It slammed so hard that the glass shattered. I knew damned well that Sanston was out of the house.

I yelled: 'You lousy rat!' and took the last five steps in one flying jump. I jerked open the front door, raced outside. I saw Sanston in his maroon Cad—at the wheel. Then two shots roared in the night.

I ducked, thinking Sanston was firing at me. But I didn't hear any slugs whistling past my ears. Then I noticed something queer. Sanston wasn't trying to step on his starter, get his car under way. He was sort of slumped over his wheel.

Dave Donaldson caught up with me. We both jumped for the maroon Cad, yanked its front door open. I said: 'What the hell!'

Sanston was bleeding at the mouth—great, crimson gushes of blood spewing out of him. He coughed once. A nasty sound, the bloody cough of a dying man. Then he shuddered, stiffened and went limp.

Donaldson looked at the gun in Sanston's relaxed hand where it rested on the upholstered seat. The gun which Sanston had carried with him out of Kitty Calvert's boudoir. A trickle of smoke curled up from the gat's muzzle. Donaldson said:'God! He shot himself!'

I said: 'Yeah. Maybe.'

'What do you mean, maybe?'

I said: 'Well, maybe he didn't commit suicide. Maybe he was murdered.'

Donaldson looked at me. 'Are you bug-house?'

'No. I don't think so. I'm just trying to figure a couple of things out. Listen—suppose Sanston told us the truth a minute ago. Suppose he was in Kitty's house, making whoopee with her. And suppose he left her for a minute to get a drink of water or see a dog about a man. And suppose while he was gone, Kitty was shot?'

'You mean maybe she really killed herself and he walked in and picked up the roscoe where she'd dropped it?'

I said: 'Don't be dense, Dave. You didn't see any powder-burns on Kitty Calvert, did you?'

'No. Come to think of it, I didn't.'

'Well, then, she didn't shoot herself.'

Donaldson said: 'Well, hell! It was Sanston that killed her. Now he's bumped himself off because he realised he was caught red-handed.'

I said: 'Not so fast. You heard Sanston say something about his wife? He didn't want to be arrested, because his wife would divorce him and the scandal would make him lose his movie job?'

Dave narrowed his eyes. 'By God! You think it was Sanston's wife—?'

I pointed towards the side of Kitty Calvert's house. I said: 'Take a look. There's a ladder up against the house. It's right up against Kitty's boudoir window.'

Donaldson said: 'I get it! Mrs Sanston followed her hubby here, saw him with Kitty Calvert, and shot Kitty. But she didn't have a chance to shoot her husband too, because he was out of the room a minute, and when he came back we busted in. So she laid for him out here by his car. Huh?'

'At least that's a theory,' I said. 'It matches with the ladder against the window.'

Dave said: 'Then we've got to get Mrs Sanston, by God! Maybe she's still around here somewhere. Come on—let's start searching!'

Even as he spoke, I heard the sound of a motor roaring from somewhere around the next corner. I said: 'If it was Mrs Sanston, she's making her getaway right now. She'll probably go home to establish an alibi for herself.'

'Alibi, hell!' Dave Donaldson roared. 'I'll catch her! I'll put the collar on her and sweat the truth out of her!'

I said: 'Go ahead. Use my jalopy. I'll go back in the house and phone headquarters to come and take the two corpses away.'

So Dave got into my coupé and got going.

I went back into the house. I picked up the phone, notified headquarters what had happened. When I hung up, I thought I heard somebody tiptoeing in the back of the place. Funny thing about people trying to sneak around without making any noise. You'll notice it quicker than you'll notice ordinary footsteps.

I made a flying dive for the dining-room where I'd heard the sound. Then I saw the Chink maid. She was trying to get out through a French window.

I jumped for her, grabbed her. She was trying to stuff something down the neck of her dress. I got my fingers into the vee of her uniform and yanked. The material tore. I ripped at the bosom of her dress until something fluttered to the floor. I grabbed it. It was an oblong of yellow paper.

The Chink girl tried to grab it from me. I slapped her across the face, pinioned her slim wrists with one hand. Then I looked at the slip of yellow paper. It was a cheque. It was made out to Miss Violet Chang, and it was signed: 'Rodney Arkle.' That had been Skinny Arkle's real name. The cheque was for five hundred smacks.

I said: 'Where the hell did you get this?'

'Mr Arkle g-gave it to me two or three d-days ago,' she whimpered. She looked scared as hell.

I said: 'What for?'

She closed up like a clam. Her red lips got tight. I knew I'd have to pull the caveman stuff on her to find out anything. So I grabbed her shoulders, shook her until her teeth rattled.

I said: 'Now look, Miss Violet Chang. If you don't want to get mauled groggy, you'll talk. How would you like a good punch in the jaw?'

'No—no—! Don't hit me!'

'Okay, then. Answer me. Why were you trying to sneak out that window?'

She said: 'Be-because I'm afraid! I don't want to get mixed up in this case.'

I ran my fingers over her shoulder, pretended I was about to pinch hell out of her. I'll admit I got something of a kick out of touching her. But I didn't let on. I said: 'Why are you afraid to get mixed up in the case?'

All of a sudden the slant-eyed cutie pressed herself up against me, put her arms around my neck. She said: 'Please, Mr Detective—I'll do anything you ask if you'll keep me out of this! I—I have a brother who was smuggled into this country illegally. If I'm dragged into this shooting, the police will question me, look into my family. They might find out about my brother and deport him—'

She fitted against me like tissue paper. Warm, soft curves were touching my chest, and she was offering me her lips—

Well, after all, I'm human. So I leaned down and kissed her . . . felt her lips part against my mouth. My blood was racing, way out of control . . .

It was some time later when I said: 'Okay, baby. Now that you know I'm your friend, maybe you'll answer a couple of questions, huh?'

'Such as what?' she asked me.

I said: 'Well, for one thing, how long had Billy Sanston been intimate with your mistress, Kitty Calvert? How long had he been coming to visit her?'

'A—a long time. Almost a year. N-now let me go, please—!'

'Not yet. Tell me something else. Did Kitty know Billy's wife?'

'Y-yes. Just slightly. They weren't good friends. Sometimes I got the impression that Mrs Sanston suspected her husband of being in love with Miss Calvert. Of course I wasn't sure. Now please let me get away—before the police come!'

Outside, in the distance, I heard sirens moaning. I said: 'Sure, kiddo.

Put on a coat to cover yourself. Then scram out the window.'

She got a coat and I held it for her. I fumbled the job, killing time. Then finally I helped her out through the French window in the dining-room, just as the headquarters men rang the front door-bell.

I raced for the hall, yelled through the broken glass in the door. I said: 'Quick—around the side! A Chink dame on the lam! Grab her!'

Those coppers moved fast. I heard them running round the side of the house. That was what I wanted.

For a minute I was alone. I set fire to a gasper and went upstairs. I didn't know what I was going to look for, but I figured maybe I might find something. I had three murders on my mind: Skinny Arkle's, his wife's, and Billy Sanston's. I was convinced they were all murders; and I had a hunch they were linked together some way or other.

First I squinted around the boudoir where Kitty Calvert's corpse was. Then I walked into the next bedroom. It had been Skinny Arkle's room. I saw a desk-drawer open.

I saw an old book of faded press-clippings from the days when Skinny had been a big-shot comedian. There were pictures of him in costume and in everyday dress. There was even a picture of Skinny as a kid with his family, back in Jugoslavia. It showed his mother, father, grand-parents, a brother exactly the same age, two older sisters, and a couple of uncles and aunts. But I didn't take the scrap-book. It was too big, too bulky.

Then I found an empty book of cheque-stubs. I looked at the last three stubs. One showed that cheque for five yards drawn to the Chink maid, Violet Chang. The second said: 'Pasadena Hospital, $250.00, in full.' The third was to cash—for fifty grand!

Before I could look around any further, I heard a hell of a rumpus down below. The headquarters men had put the nab on the Chinese girl. I didn't want them to catch me going through Skinny Arkle's things, so I went downstairs on the run. I said: 'You guys better take that girl to the jug. I think she knows something. And how about lending me a car for a while? Dave Donaldson took my hack.'

One of the dicks said: 'All right. Use the red roadster, Mr Turner. Run it back to headquarters when you get through with it.'

I went out, got into the red roadster. I drove back to my apartment. Just as I parked outside my building, I saw somebody in the entrance. Somebody in a suit that looked familiar.

It was one of my own suits!

I said: 'What the hell!' and jumped for the guy. I grabbed him. Only it wasn't a him; it was a her. It was the blonde bimbo, Constance Calvert.

She fought at me. She said: 'Damn you! Let me go!'

'Like hell!' I told her. 'How long have you been out of my place?'

'I—I just got out. I found a suit of yours and put it on. Why did you take my clothes?'

Before I could answer her, I heard brakes squeaking. I turned. There was Dave Donaldson driving up in my jalopy. He jumped out, saw me holding the blonde dame. He said: 'What—?'

'Put the nippers on this girl, Dave,' I told him. 'She's hard to hold.'

Dave slipped the cuffs on her. Then he said: 'Turner, I've got news!'

I said: 'What kind of news?'

'Well, in the first place,' Donaldson growled disgustedly, 'Mrs Sanston had a perfect alibi. She's been playing bridge with friends all evening. Hasn't been outdoors. That eliminates her as a suspect. But down at headquarters I found out something damned interesting. Billy Sanston had been married before. His first wife's name was Nancy Norward. Ever hear of her?'

I said: 'Good God! Nancy Norward was the girl who died down in San Diego on a party with Skinny Arkle.'

Dave said: 'Yeah. Now do you see the set-up? Sanston must have nursed a grudge against Arkle all these years. To get even he played around with Kitty Calvert, Arkle's wife. Then, finally, he bumped Arkle off and decapitated the body. Maybe Kitty found out about it, so he had to kill her too. Then when we busted in on him in Kitty's boudoir he committed suicide. There was no other way out.'

I said: 'Dave, maybe you're right. It all checks up pretty well. Except one thing. Why was Arkle's severed head sent to me?'

'I don't know that,' Donaldson grunted. 'And there's one other goofy point, too. The medical examiner's report says that the bullet was fired into Arkle's noggin *after he was dead*! The condition of the tissues, or something. Look—here's the report.'

He handed me a sheet of paper. I let him hang onto Constance while I took the paper to a street-light. It was the usual formal report of the medical examiner—the description of the bullet-wound, condition of the flesh, colour of the hair and eyes, so many fillings in the teeth, and the way the head had evidently been sliced from the body itself. I read it over once. And then, suddenly, I had the answer.

I jumped back towards Donaldson. I said: 'Quick! Get in my hack! We'll take this dame with us. And we've got to move fast!'

Dave said: 'Where the hell are we headed?'

'Pasadena!' I told him. 'The Pasadena Hospital!'

It took us just thirty minutes to make the trip, and I thumbed my nose at a dozen stop-signs on the way. I jerked all the tread off my tyres skidding to a stop outside the Pasadena Hospital, and I grabbed Donaldson's arm. 'Come on!' I yelled.

'What about this dame?' He pointed to Constance Calvert.

'Leave her here in my hack. She's handcuffed.' I shoved Donaldson into the hospital and we went up to the desk.

There was an elderly woman on duty. I said: 'I want to see a record of the deaths in this place during the past three days.' Dave Donaldson flashed his badge for authority.

The woman dug into her records, handed me four or five cards. I found the one I wanted. It said: 'Rodney Arkellmeister. Age 48. Male. White. Entered hospital in dying condition. Pneumonia. Unable to talk. Died two days later . . .' Then it gave the date of death and all that stuff.

I whirled on Donaldson. 'Get it?' I said. 'Rodney Arkellmeister! That was Skinny Arkle's real name before he came to America from Jugoslavia.'

Dave said: 'You mean Skinny died a natural death? Then who the hell cut off his head and put a bullet in it? Who sent the head to you?'

Before I could answer him, I heard a scream from outside. A woman's scream. I said: 'What the hell—!' and jumped for the door. I saw a car parked behind my coupé. There was a guy leaning in my hack. He was choking Constance Calvert.

I said: 'Damn! He must have been lurking around my apartment-house! He heard me saying we were coming here! He followed us!' And I hurled myself at the guy.

He heard me. He turned. I saw a roscoe in his fist. It vomited flame. A slug zinged past my skull. I whipped out my own automatic, thumbed the safety, squeezed the trigger. I sent three slugs into the guy's guts.

Even before he fell I yelled out to Donaldson. I said: 'There's your killer. It's Skinny Arkle!'

Dave said: 'You're crazy! How can a headless corpse get up and walk around—?'

By that time I was kneeling over the fallen man. I turned him over.

It was Skinny Arkle, all right. I'd have known his face anywhere. Especially after seeing the decapitated head drop in my lap earlier that night, in my apartment.

Donaldson stared. He said: 'Good God!'

I reached down, shoved my fingers in Skinny Arkle's mouth. I twisted—and pulled out his false teeth. I said: 'Well, that proves it, Skinny.'

Arkle glared up at me. His eyes were beginning to glaze. He said: 'Damn you—!'

I said: 'I see the whole thing now. You were the murderer, Arkle. You knew your wife, Kitty Calvert, was intimate with her director, Billy Sanston. You got proof of your suspicions from your wife's Chink maid, Violet Chang. You gave her your cheque for five hundred clams for telling you the low-down.'

Skinny Arkle gurgled in his throat and vomited a little blood from his punctured guts.

I said: 'By sheer luck, your brother had just come to visit you from Jugoslavia. *Your twin brother!* You and he were identical twins; looked exactly alike. I saw a picture of you two in your scrap-book a while ago.

'It showed you and your twin as kids back in the old country. You looked alike even in those days.'

Dave Donaldson said: 'I'll be damned!'

I went on talking to Skinny Arkle. 'When your brother got to Holly-wood, he was already stricken with pneumonia. You knew he was going to die. You saw a swell chance to murder your chiselling wife and her lover without being suspected of the crime. So you had your brother brought here to Pasadena—to a hospital. He died here. You arranged his burial somewhere—then you exhumed his corpse and cut its head off, put a bullet in it as a blind. That was the head you sent to me!'

Arkle said: 'Ar-r-r-gh—!'

'You sent your twin brother's severed head to me, knowing I'd call the cops and notify them you'd been murdered. Then, tonight, you put a ladder outside your wife's boudoir and climbed up. You shot her and threw the gun on the bed alongside her, to make it look like suicide. Maybe you'd have shot Billy Sanston at the same time, but he'd gone into the next room.

'Then when Donaldson and I broke in, you saw that Sanston would be accused of murdering Kitty Calvert—and probably convicted. So you sneaked down the ladder, satisfied. But a moment later, Billy Sanston escaped. So you shot him with a second gun you had on you. You shot him as he got into his Cad. That made it look as if Sanston, too, was a suicide.'

Donaldson stared at me. 'How the hell did you guess?'

I said: 'I knew, the minute you showed me the medical examiner's report of that severed head. It mentioned several fillings in the teeth. And I knew that the real Skinny Arkle *had false teeth*! He used to take them out and fold up his face, in the movies! Then I remembered that cheque-stub I'd seen in Arkle's book—a cheque made out to the Pasadena Hospital. I realised the truth. Arkle had done the killings, and now he'd probably try to escape by going back to Jugoslavia on his dead brother's passport.'

Dave Donaldson leaned over Skinny Arkle, felt in his pockets. He brought out a passport and a steamship ticket. That cinched the thing.

Skinny Arkle's eyes fluttered. He mumbled: 'Well—Turner . . . they won't—hang me . . . you took . . . care of that . . . damn you . . .' A spew of crimson gushed out of his kisser, and he folded up. And that was the end of Skinny Arkle.

Then I remembered Constance Calvert. She was slumped over in my jalopy. Arkle must have followed us; and maybe she'd spotted him. Anyhow, he'd tried to murder her quietly; probably figured on bumping Donaldson and me, too, when we came out of the hospital. He must have known the jig was up. But I wasn't thinking about Skinny Arkle any more. I was thinking of the blonde Calvert wren.

She'd been choked unconscious; but she wasn't seriously hurt. I turned to Dave Donaldson. I said: 'Dave, you stay here and notify the Pasadena police—have them take Skinny's carcass away.'

Dave said: 'Where are you going?'

I said: 'Well, I left this girl's clothes in my apartment earlier tonight. So now I'm going to take her back to get 'em.'

'Hell!' Donaldson growled. 'I'll bet you won't hurry about it.'

I said: 'You flatter me, Dave.' But it turned out that he was right, at that!

CARROLL JOHN DALY

Carroll John Daly was born in Yonkers, New York in 1889. Educated at the American Academy of Dramatic Arts, he studied acting and ran a number of movie theatres before turning to writing. In 1922, with the publication of 'The False Burton Combs' in *Black Mask* magazine, Daly created the prototype of the hard-boiled private eye. However, it was his story 'Knights of the Open Palm', published in 1923, again in *Black Mask* that magazine, which is seen as founding the genre of hard-boiled detective fiction. It featured the first appearance of Race Williams, a twin-pistol toting detective with an acerbic wit and strict code of honour, who went on to feature in eight of Daly's novels and a number of short stories. Williams is now seen as establishing the model for the countless hard-boiled private eyes who would feature in magazines throughout the twenties and thirties. Daly's novel *The Snarl of the Beast*, published in 1927, also featuring Race Williams, is now seen as the first private eye novel ever published. Towards the end of his writing career, Daly had a number of fallings-out with *Black Mask*'s editorial staff. During the thirties and forties, his work was somewhat overshadowed by that of Dashiell Hammett, and Daly eventually faded into relative obscurity. He died in Los Angeles, California.

DASHIELL HAMMETT

Dashiell Hammett was in Southern Maryland, USA in 1894. He grew up in Philadelphia and Baltimore, before leaving school at thirteen to work with a variety of companies, including the Pinkerton National Detective Agency, with whom he served as an operative between 1915 and 1922. It was the experiences he had while there which provided much of the inspiration for his fiction.

Hammett turned to writing in the twenties – his first published story, 'The Gatewood Caper' (1923), is one of the earliest examples of hardboiled crime fiction – and by the middle of that decade was the pre-eminent writer of detective fiction in America. During the twenties and thirties produced Hammett five novels and a raft of short fiction. Arguably his most successful works – both critically and commercially – are *Red Harvest* (1929), *The Dain Curse* (1929), and *The Glass Key* (1931). *Red Harvest* was included by *Time* magazine its '100 Best English-language Novels from 1923 to 2005' feature, and Nobel Prize-winning French author André Gide described the novel as "a remarkable achievement, the last word in atrocity, cynicism, and horror."

Hammett's later life was marked in part by ill health, alcoholism, a period of imprisonment related to his alleged membership in the American Communist Party, and by his troubled relationship with his long-time companion, the author Lillian Hellman. He wrote less and less, and by the fifties had become something of a hermit. In 1961, Hammett died in a New York City hospital of lung cancer, diagnosed just two months before. His legacy is formidable: James Ellroy declared that "great crime fiction started with Hammett," and Tony Hillerman called him "the most important American mystery writer of the twentieth century."

ROBERT LESLIE BELLEM

Robert Leslie Bellem was born in 1902, probably in Los Angeles, USA. He worked as a journalist, radio announcer, and film extra, before turning to writing in his late twenties. Bellem started publishing his stories in pulp magazines around 1935; writing in a variety of genres, it is estimated that he produced some 3000 short stories in a career lasting less than 30 years. His most famous creation was the hardboiled Hollywood detective Dan Turner, whose first appearance was in the second issue of *Spicy Detective*, dated June 1934. Bellem also wrote at least two novels, of which the best-known is *Blue Murder* (1938).

www.ingramcontent.com/pod-product-compliance
Lightning Source LLC
Chambersburg PA
CBHW020731250626
47155CB00006B/2255